DIVINE DECEPTION

- The Divine Chronicles Book 6 -

JoAnna Grace

ABW-WJP, LLC
P.O. Box 337
Lindale, TX 75771

2022 Cover Design by Moorbooks Design
Book design by Champagne Book Design
Printed in the United States of America

Library of Congress Control Number Data
Grace, JoAnna.
Divine Deception / JoAnna Grace.
1. Fantasy romance—greek mythology—Fiction. 2. Romance—Fantasy—Fiction.
3. Sagas—Romance—Fiction.
Fiction. | BISAC: FICTION / Romance / Fantasy. | FICTION / Romance / General. | FICTION / Sagas.
ISBN 978-1-951594-01-5
ISBN 978-1-951594-00-8 (e-book)
www.authorjoannagrace.com

JoAnna Grace

CONTEMPORARY ROMANCES

The Roles We Play

Riverview Romances

Why The River Runs

A River Between Us

PARANORMAL TITLES

Divine Chronicle Series:

Divine Awakening

Divine Destiny

Divine Judgment

Divine Encounter

Divine Pursuit

Divine Deception

Divine Justice

Blake Pride Series:

Pride Before the Fall

Break Her Fall

The Harder They Fall

Divided We Fall

Rise After the Fall

For more information on JoAnna's books, signings, events, and more,
Sign up for the NEWSLETTER at http://eepurl.com/B_DM5!

A Note From Jo

Thank you, dear readers, for once again picking up a JoAnna
Grace novel. I hope you enjoy it. It brings me great joy to hear
from you. Please connect with me on social media:

Facebook: facebook.com/joannagraceauthor
Instagram: instagram.com/authorjoannagrace

Want updates delivered to your inbox?
Make sure you're in the know.
Sign up for my newsletter today! Visit http://eepurl.
com/B_DM5

Do you want to help an author?

Leave a review!

Your opinion matters. Every review can help.

Share a link to this book on social media!

Like, follow, tag Jo, and share this book with your friends.

Support Indie Authors!

Did you know that an Indie Author fronts all

the cost of production?

That's right. We appreciate every person who purchases

our books because that's how we continue to produce

more. Independent authors, cover designers, editors, and

formatters work hard to bring readers quality products and

stories they can fall in love with.

Like. Share. Follow. Subscribe. Tag. Review.

It all helps the Indie community!

Share the Love.

A note to the reader

Ariabella's journey began before Avery McClain ever met Ryse Castille, before her beloved little brother, Dante, was taken as one of Avery's guardians. Back then, Dante and Ariabella exchanged a series of letters discussing everything from what his life was like at the Thracian Training Center in Tennessee to her life in Trastevere, Italy near the Roman Haven where they grew up.

What I hope you enjoy about Ariabella's story is her perspective on so many events that have happened in previous Divine Chronicles books. The events of this story run parallel to *Divine Destiny*, *Divine Judgement*, and *Divine Pursuit* and lead up to the next full-length installment of the Divine Chronicles, where all the characters are together in their fight against evil.

Thanks to:

I want to say a very special thanks to Cinzia, my OWG sister and source of Italian! Her help with the language was priceless and she truly aided in putting the finishing touches on Ariabella's native language. *Grazie sorella mi!* I learned so much through this process and I hope that you, the reader, feel like you've stepped into Rome! Any incorrect terms are my fault, not hers.

Thanks to everyone who helped make this book what it is: Carol, Beth, Jen, and Stacey. I have the most wonderful team in you ladies. I appreciate you sharing your talents. A HUGE thank you, Meg Murrey, for creating the most stunning bonus images for this series. Her original concept for this cover is the inspiration for all the new covers.. Love you!

As always, thanks to my family, who put up with Mommy constantly at the computer and having conversations with my imaginary friends. Thanks, D, for the hot date nights that end up in the appliance section at Lowes and for celebrating with me every time I finish a book. Thanks Mom and Cheryl for constantly listening to me while I verbally plot, vent, brag, and bitch about the people in my head. I love you all so very much!!!

CHAPTER ONE

Trastevere, Italy

A RIABELLA CLUTCHED THE PHONE TO HER EAR AND SPOKE ENGLISH as clearly as she could. "I can't believe you call me, *cosa cè fratelleino*. Something is wrong?"

Dante, her little brother currently staying in America, sighed into the phone. "I needed to hear your voice." His Italian accent wasn't nearly as pronounced as hers, though it was there, hiding under the American muck. Unlike Dante, she'd lived in Roma her entire life, over eighty years, though you'd never know by looking at her. Olympians didn't age like humans, thank the gods. No one would guess her to be a day over twenty-five.

Ariabella sat down on her balcony. The apartment was prime

real estate overlooking the River Tiber and the sidewalk cafes below. The waters flowed through her veins right along with her Olympian blood. She loved this part of Roma. Over the decades, she'd lived in every part of her home country. Trastevere was her favorite so far. "I am always here *per te. Sempre.*" She loved their written correspondences, seeing his handwriting and touching paper that he put his pen to. Olympian mail was much more efficient than the humans' snail mail, taking only seconds to leave his postal station and arrive at hers for delivery. "You like to be Thracian? Is good?"

"*Si, si bene.*" The lackluster emotion behind the words felt stale in her ears.

"*Lo sai,* you cannot lie to me, Dante."

He groaned. "You're not supposed to use your powers on me."

Ariabella grinned at his irritation. "I don't have to, *lo sento*! I hear it; I know you."

"Yes, you do. Which is why I'm calling, there are things happening here *sorella mia*, strange and unusual things for sure. I need to know you're safe. I need to know you're being careful."

A quick glance at her watch spoke of more. If it was ten in the morning in Italy, then Dante was calling at four in the morning from the Haven in America.

"Dante, not make me ask. No need for my powers to understand; it is very early in America. *Hai paura,* you scared? *Perchè?*

"The Avondales arrived a couple days ago. Father came. Did you know about this?"

"*Si.* I'm sorry to hear about the death of your Lady Avery and Grand Deity Troy. *Mi spiace.* He was an honorable man and she was kind to you, based on your letters." It was a day that shook the Olympian population around the world. Their race were not immortals like the gods. All the same, they were capable of living many centuries. For a Grand Deity to be murdered was unheard of. Troy Castille was only one rung below the gods on the Olympian food chain and he had been taken down by poison at his son's mating ceremony. It was only made worse when another Deity Princess, Ariabella's countryman, had murdered a Divine Grace—the woman who had given Dante a true purpose and accepted his unique gift. The events of that day had all Olympians questioning their safety. If a Grand Deity and a Divine Grace could die so easily, no one was safe.

"Thank you. I wish I had called you with better tidings. Unfortunately, I do not."

She clenched her eyes closed. The tension between her brother and father had always been thick. "Has *Papà* done something?"

"He…" Dante took a deep breath, and firmed up his tone. "We argued and he struck me."

"*Cosa?*" Ariabella sat up, her coffee nearly spilling from the cup. "Why would he do that?"

"It's…complicated."

"*Cazzo.*" She spat out the curse. She didn't believe it could be too complicated for her brother to explain. Their father could be a monstrous man, they both knew it. Dante didn't have to water down things for her. "*Spiegati*, explain."

"I… I cannot, not completely. All I can tell you is that while the Deities are ascended to the Heavens, please, Ariabella, be cautious. Trust no one, even with your gifts. Things are not as they seem with Father and I'm afraid of what he might do to you if he knows we are in contact. Call Bridget, warn her. Check on the other girls and *Mamma*, please, for me."

Xavier had made his declaration to the family years ago.

Dante was a Thracian. He was a soldier, a killer, not their baby brother to be coddled and loved. The ten girls that preceded him were not allowed to spoil him and make him soft. Ariabella, and her closest sister, Bridget, the two eldest, couldn't stay away from their *fratello*, though. He was their joy, their laughter, their baby. Mother had raised him the best she could according to their father's wishes. They all loved Dante and doted on him behind Xavier's back. Now, decades later, Ariabella still favored her brother above all others, which was why she and Bridget had left the safety of the Roman Haven to live in the human world. They wanted to be free. Xavier's strict rules were not unjust or without their cause; they simply didn't appeal to her any longer. Ariabella, Dante, and Bridget were adults and could make their own decisions as to how to treat one another.

"Father wouldn't hurt us, Dante. We're his children."

"You are. I'm not. Not any longer. And Father is the least of my worries at present. I have to go. No matter what happens, I love you very much, Aria."

"*Santo Zeus,* Dante. Does this have to do with the murder of the Grand Deity? Is there more to it?" She didn't want him to hang up so fast. His voice held fear and worry.

"Yes, but… There is no time. I must go. I love you, big sister."

"*A presto, fratellino.*" Ariabella's heart broke at the sadness in his tone. Dante possessed such a gentle soul, despite his Thracian blood. He couldn't live in the human world like she did. Those sand-colored eyes and his massive body would draw too much attention. The light shade of brown in his eyes was radiant, though unnatural for humans.

Her eyes scanned the tops of the other buildings in the city and across the river. What in the name of the gods was going on with their world that her brother had to call and check on her?

His call only left her with more questions instead of answers. What did he mean, "no matter what"? What could be worse than Rogues? He didn't know the details of her investigatory job, so he couldn't be referring to anything that she had going on in the human world. Ariabella twirled a strand of her blonde hair around her fingers as she contemplated Dante's call and all the prior information in his letters.

Dante's warning tickled the back of her mind. *Trust no one.* Truth was to Ariabella like the tide was to the moon. She could pull it out of people, take it, if she wanted to. With her gifts, no one could deceive her, Olympian or otherwise. She tucked all this information aside to examine later. She needed to review her files and prepare for tomorrow.

The next morning, she made her way an hour north from Roma. She was hot on the trail of a man involved with human trafficking and the police only called her in when they were desperate—like now.

Ariabella smiled at the man across the interrogation table from her. She met his eyes without hesitation and held his stare. She had no reason to be nervous. But if this poor sod had the misfortune of being placed in front of her, he surely did.

Their suspect would never recognize her outside of this room. Ariabella had become Jane, her alias. Jane had long, dark hair and light brown eyes. She wore black suits a few sizes larger than Ariabella, thanks to a padded body suit. The disguise had worked for years. Even the police were used to seeing it.

Beside her sat an interpreter, her longtime partner, Edgar. Ariabella could understand English as her second language. Part of her tactics kept that knowledge in the dark when dealing with Americans. She turned to Edgar and spoke only in Italian. "Would you please introduce us?" she asked, only to see if their suspect could understand Italian.

When she spoke, the suspect's eyes darted from her breasts, which weren't anything to gawk at, in her opinion, and back to her lips. He scowled. "She can't speak English?"

Edgar nodded and turned to the suspect and spoke in aristocratically proper English. "It's not her native tongue. My name is Edgar. This is my associate, Jane. We are here to ask you a few questions. Please answer, no matter how trivial the subject. It helps her get a more precise read on you." Edgar's wide, friendly smile stretched across his dark-skinned face. The pair of them had worked together for years and they had the ruse down to a science.

The suspect, a typical white male with prison tats on his knuckles, eyed Ariabella, raising one brow and frowning. "Who the hell is she?" He once again flickered his eyes to her chest. "She looks like a damn schoolteacher, not a Fed. What's she gonna do? Teach me the alphabet?" He snickered and rolled his eyes, brushing her off with little more than the shake of his head.

"Can you please state your name?" Edgar asked, completely ignoring his inquiry.

"Al Smith."

Bugiardo! Lie. Ariabella pressed her lips together, kept her façade, and looked to Edgar, speaking in Italian, "That was the most unoriginal, unimpressive alias ever. Not his legal name, even though it was on all his international travel paperwork."

The suspect clearly didn't understand what she had said. "Don't you know that already? You people seem incredibly uninformed."

Edgar took a deep breath and once again addressed the

suspect. "Sir, please cooperate. It's in your best interest. Now please tell me what color your shirt is."

"Is she color blind too?" A nerve in his upper lip twitched at his smart remark. When no one else found it humorous, he swallowed.

Ariabella glanced to Edgar for interpretation. Edgar shook his head, as if to say that the retort was not worth the effort to interpret.

"Without the sarcasm, sir. Keep in mind our testimony can either add to your innocence or put the final nail in your coffin. You're getting off on the wrong foot."

The suspect's nostrils flared and his jaw clenched. Yes, he needed Ariabella and Edgar on his side. He averted his eyes and nodded, resigned to cooperating. "My shirt is green."

Ariabella listened to Edgar's interpretation and nodded. "Ask him to talk about his siblings. Anything he can remember."

Edgar went back and forth, reversing the languages between Ariabella and the suspect.

He had two sisters. One died of an overdose last year. The other moved to Nebraska after that and he hadn't seen her since. Again, the nerve in his upper lip tweaked. This was a physical response when he was disgusted with something. She noted it.

Vero. True. Ariabella's internal gifts whispered into her mind. She had much more than years of human intelligence training at work. "When did he come to Italy?"

The suspect paused, looked to the ceiling, back to her boobs, and answered, "Three weeks ago."

Vero. "What was the purpose of your trip?"

He shrugged; his eyes flickered to Edgar. "I came to see the sights."

Falso. "What sights has he seen since his arrival?"

"You know, that big arena thing. And the naked people statues. It's Rome. There's a lot to see."

Bugia. "Ask him how he enjoyed the Colosseum."

"What does this have to do with my case? It was big rock bowl, okay?" He leaned his elbows on the table and stared at Ariabella. That telling nerve twitched again. "Why don't you just do what you need to do to get me out of this country?"

Edgar transferred his message to Ariabella and she pressed her lips together, narrowing her eyes at the man. It didn't matter how many stupid, meaningless questions she was forced to ask him; she already knew he was guilty. She merely had to get him to say the right words that the detective needed him to say.

Ariabella nodded and prattled in Italian, "Fine. Where were you on August fourteenth, between the hours of 4:00PM and 8:00PM?"

"I was shopping," he boldly lied and even met her eyes when he did it. Suddenly, when he had to focus on his answer, he had no interest in her breasts. "There's a market—"

"That market was closed. We've established that, sir." Edgar didn't let it pass. "We have police verification it closed due to weather. Try again."

The pale skin of the suspect's hand contrasted with the inky black hair he ran it through. "Hmm, yeah, yeah. I remember. It was storming. I think I hit a pub to get out of the rain."

"Were any of these women at that pub?" Edgar motioned for Ariabella to hand him the pictures of the missing girls. All were Olympian, all of them in their twenties, and all of them were supposedly dead or missing—as far as they knew.

He went through the pictures one by one, commenting on how ugly or hot each one was. "Sorry, boss. No luck," he pointed at one blond, "but she's pretty smoking. If you have her number…"

"She's dead." Edgar gathered the photos. Ariabella watched for any reaction from her mark.

"Ouch." He grimaced and blew out a deep breath. "Tough break. She should've had a man like me around to protect her."

Edgar snapped back at him fast, "She was kidnapped, along with these other women, for a trafficking ring. Hers is the only body we've found. She was beaten and abused in ways I don't need to describe in mixed company."

"I don't treat women like that. It's sick." There was no twitching in his lip. His disapproval wasn't genuine. He also pointedly stared at Ariabella's eyes.

Edgar interpreted and Ariabella continued her questioning. "Do you know Julio Val D'Esta?"

"Can't say I do." Al Smith leaned back in the chair and crossed his arms over his chest, and the foot stopped tapping under the table. His eyes were alert, and his breathing had steadied, setting a purposeful pace, yet he spoke the truth.

Edgar produced a picture of the suspect shaking hands with a known associate of Val D'Esta. "And this man you seem to know well. Who is he?"

Al nodded at the picture. "That's McGrath. I don't know any Julio whatever."

Vero. Which meant McGrath was another protective layer of Val D'Esta's network.

"What is your business with McGrath?" Edgar asked on his own. He relayed the answer to Ariabella. "Says he's trying to get into the nightclub business and came here for pointers."

Bugia. No, not a full lie, but a half-lie.

They volleyed back and forth, asking more questions and

getting more half-truths and rehearsed answers. Nothing they could use to verify that this guy was Julio Val D'Esta's new trafficking partner in America. Only rubbish about nightclubs and business plans. In her opinion, McGrath had made a mistake in his choice. Al was one evolutionary step above walking on all fours.

It seemed like they questioned him for over an hour before Edgar finally sighed and closed his notebook. His signal. "If we're going to continue like this, I'm going to need more coffee," he said to Al in English. He spoke in Italian to Ariabella, asking her if she wanted a refill.

She grinned kindly and handed him the tumbler. Al Smith's ankles were cuffed to the floor; she was in no danger being alone with him while Edgar stepped out.

Ariabella wrote notes, acting like she was documenting some pertinent information. All the while, Al's feet would twitch right along with his upper lip.

"Whatcha writing, pretty lady?"

Ariabella prattled off in Italian about how she didn't understand and they shouldn't speak while Edgar was gone. Then she smiled and turned her attention back to her notes. A few minutes later, she checked her watch and sighed with impatience. Ariabella thumbed through her notes, acting as if she weren't aware of every minute move the suspect made.

"*Humph.*" Al leaned back and his lips curved. "It's too bad we hadn't met outside of this place. I'd like to see if you taste as sweet as you look." He spoke softly, clearly not thinking there were multiple microphones in the room. "Then I'd pass you around. Boss man said the young-looking ones go for more than the older ones. You're just ripe for the picking."

Giving him her most innocent, wide-eyed look of confusion,

Ariabella crinkled her brow as if she didn't understand a word of what he was saying, being as she was simply a cute, naive little lady and all. She said the first few words of an old Italian song, testing once more if he knew a shred of her native tongue.

Clueless in every way, this one.

Al huffed a cocky laugh and relaxed in his chair, once again bouncing his knee and staring at her breasts. "Whatever, babe." They sat in silence for a few more moments and he finally broke. "You know, one phone call is all it would take to get you on the line, right up there on the buffet with the other girls. Fat, rich bastards would pay good money to get their hands on you. You'd earn me a pretty penny. I mean, your tits could use some help, but some guys like that flat-chested look. Once I get set up in the States, I hope to get lots of bitches like you running through the back. McGrath will be so proud." He sneered the last sentence and Ariabella smiled in return.

"Thank you, Mr. Smith," Ariabella said in English, her *th* coming out as an *s* sound in her heavy accent. "That is precisely what I needed to hear."

He sat straight up in his chair, his face turning whiter by the second. "You lying sack of sh—"

Ariabella pushed a fraction of her power towards the suspect and said the words that could damn any guilty party. "Al Smith, tell me the truth. Are you in cooperation with de man you call McGrath in a trafficking ring?"

"Yes, I mean, not yet. *Shit!*" He slapped his hands over his mouth and his eyes rounded in shock.

Ariabella pulled out the picture of the suspect shaking McGrath's hand. Her English was choppy, so she had to enunciate to be clear. "Is dis the man you know as McGrath?"

"Yes." He slammed his hand down table. "You're a bloody witch!"

"No, sir, I am investigator." Ariabella calmly showed him more pictures as his anxiety hit the roof. His eyes twitched, his leg bounced under the table like a jackhammer, his fingers drummed on the table.

"Is this McGrath speaking to Val D'Esta?" McGrath leaned against a black SUV speaking to the man inside. The face of the illusive Val D'Esta was cleverly hidden in the shadow of the car.

"I told you I don't know who Val D'Esta is. McGrath takes orders from someone who drives a car like that, though."

Al Smith's wide eyes studied her hard, as if seeing her for the first time. She used some of her aura to blur her face so he would have a hard time recalling the shape of her nose or the curve of her lips.

"You said you don't speak English."

"No, he say is not my true language. No lie. There is difference." She winked at Al Smith and knew that Edgar was collecting their check as she made the man confess all his sins. "Now, you must tell me where he is."

"I can't. If I knew that, I'd go find him myself and warn him about *you*."

Ariabella frowned and tilted her head sideways. "Dat was hurtful. Is not my fault you bla bla around pretty women." She gathered her notes and files, stood, and gave Al a head nod. "*Grazie* for your cooperation. *Ciao*." She exited the room to Al screaming about a lawyer and being coerced. She paid him no attention. Any lawyer would see that he dug his grave long before she ever spoke the first word of English.

There was nothing more satisfying than the look on the lead detective's face when she came out of the room.

"I don't know how you do it. I think that guy may be right about you." He sighed and rubbed the back of his neck.

"What? That fat, rich bastards would pay good money to get their hands on me?" Ariabella pushed long black hair off her shoulders.

"No, that you're a witch. That's the fifth guy this year who has spilled his bloody guts to you when none of my other detectives could break them."

With a shrug, she adjusted the strap of her bag on her shoulder. "I have one of those faces. People tend to be very open with me. It's a real problem when I'm in a hurry." She slid on dark sunglasses before the cop noticed the contacts.

In the parking lot, Edgar gently touched her shoulder. "You'll need to lie low for a while. If the police find McGrath based on this information, Val D'Esta will find out and you'll be a target. Do you have transportation away from here?"

"Everything is taken care of. I'm not staying in the city any longer than necessary."

"Good. I'll wire your share of the money and let you know when our next appointment is."

"*Perfetto.*" They parted ways with nothing more than a nod of the head. Edgar slid into a taxi. She walked down the street and entered a restaurant about two blocks away.

Ariabella went into the bathroom, locked the door, and retrieved a duffle from the sink cabinet. Time was of the essence, so she carefully removed the black wig and contact lenses that lightened her eyes. She quickly wiped off the dark makeup, leaving her skin completely natural; nothing but sun-kissed and flawless. The padded body suit was shoved into the very bottom of her bag. Her black suit jacket and matching pants were folded neatly and tucked on top of the padding, replaced by a bright summer dress and sandals. Free from the wig, her waves of blonde hair flowed down to her waist and about her shoulders. She replaced her dark, boring black sunglasses with fun, floral printed ones and used them like a head band.

The small duffle held another bag, more vibrant and colorful. She unfolded it, stuffed the duffle inside, and zipped it closed. No one would ever know what the bag contained. She made sure that the investigator who entered the restaurant was not the same woman who exited. Instead of using the main entrance that she came through, she slipped out the side door, into the courtyard, and ordered an herbal tea. All smiles and sunshine, Ariabella waved to passersby. She sat there long enough to peruse a fashion magazine and to make sure she wasn't being followed, using her aura to covertly search for other Olympians in the area.

The cheerful blonde slid into a seemingly random vehicle and settled in for the long ride back to Trastevere. An hour into her ride, her phone pinged with the notification that a wire transfer had hit her bank.

"*Grazie*, Edgar." She smiled to herself and put the phone back in her purse. Her job paid well and there was satisfaction in helping catch criminals and setting innocents free. What she hated was going through all the farce of asking more than one question. If people would leave her alone with the suspects, all she would have to say were four words: tell me the truth.

No one could resist her powers, human or Olympian. The gods had blessed and cursed her with the truth. She knew the moment a person uttered a lie and if they wouldn't tell her the truth, all she had to do was ask. A breeze of her powers would loosen their tongues. A gust would have them confessing sins long forgotten. The curse came when someone said something untrue out of kindness.

No, you look great in that dress.

Of course he liked you.

Your boobs aren't too small.

Her human friends had no idea she knew the truth behind their words. She had learned a long time ago that it wasn't always what people said that mattered, rather the heart behind it. People told little white lies all the time to keep from hurting others. It was a socially acceptable norm. The problem rested with her, not everyone else. If she didn't have her gifts, she wouldn't know that her best human friend was terribly jealous of her tiny frame and long wavy hair. Her friend would never say an unkind word, but it was true, nonetheless, which was why Ariabella didn't keep many close friends. Being alone was often easier and a lot less stressful.

After two hours of tactically misleading driving, Ariabella arrived at her apartment. She tipped the driver well. This man had gone far out of the way in order to mislead anyone tailing them. Then again, he'd dropped her off several times before, so he knew what he was getting into when she paged him.

Home. Her apartment in Trastevere was her favorite place on earth. The space overlooked the River Tiber and was one of the only apartments in the building that had a balcony. It wasn't much, yet it was enough that she could sit in her chair and hear the water while she read.

Tonight, she drank a glass of wine and thought about the dirt bag sitting in jail thanks to her powers. Today, her gifts were a blessing. Today, she was one step closer to putting Val D'Esta behind bars too. The man was the scum of the earth, and if she could take him down, countless lives would be saved. Her stomach churned at the thought of all the young women he had killed, the families he had destroyed. Those women didn't have a chance.

Some didn't have Olympian gifts to protect them from predators like she did.

She called her friend to catch up on the last couple days and told a few lies of her own so that the girl would think she was on one of her shopping trips, not interrogating criminals. According to her human friend, Ariabella was simply a somewhat spoiled rich girl from a well-to-do family. Her entire life revolved around truth and lies. By the gods, it was exhausting.

Could she not have at least one relationship, outside of her family, where she could be completely honest?

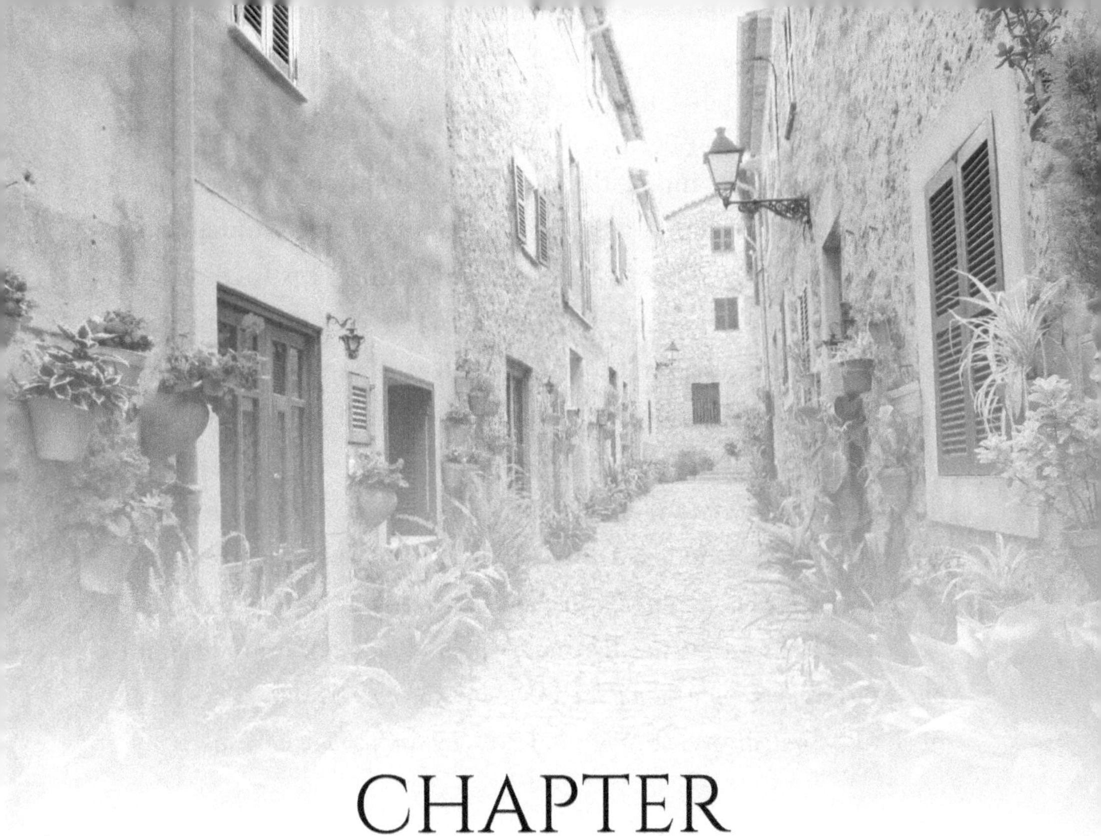

CHAPTER
TWO

RIABELLA STRODE DOWN THE COBBLESTONE STREETS, ENJOYING a warm day in Trastevere. She hummed the song stuck in her head, the one she heard in the taverna the night before. Over one arm hung a bag of groceries; in her other hand were fresh flowers to display on her dining table. It was such a lovely day, she put an extra skip in her step. A permanent smile spread across her face and she gave it away to everyone she passed on the street. In her purse was another letter from her *fratellino* in America and she couldn't wait to grab a coffee and read it.

Today, she took the long way around to her favorite *caffè* in Piazza di Santa Maria to sit and enjoy the day and read her letter. She gave the flowers an appreciative sniff before setting them on the table and settling in. The sun shone down on her bare legs and sandaled feet. The skirt was a nice choice on a day like today, as if Zeus himself was shining his love down on the world. Her heart was light and her soul was happy as she took a seat and pulled out the letter. She read about the Oracle who had come to the Haven to council the Deities and those who had lost their families.

Lysandra's beauty is like nothing I've ever beheld. I've seen lovely women before, though none who stun me. None who have made me as nervous or self-conscious as she does. What do you know of the Oracles of Delphi? I'm scouring the libraries to find out all that I can. I want to know this woman more than I've ever wanted to know anyone, even Avery. My loyalty shall always be to her, however, Lysandra may have taken my heart.

Ariabella's jaw dropped and she covered her mouth with her hand. Had her wonderful little brother found love? She closed her eyes and clutched the letter to her chest. *Dearest Zeus, let Dante find the happiness he so deserves.* Her prayers lifted to the sky and her cheeks hurt, she smiled so wide.

"I would give anything to know what put such a look on a woman's face. Men all over the world would pay loads of money for that secret."

At the table beside her sat a cute young man with big brown eyes. He leaned back in his chair, watching her, with his hands wrapped around a book. His Italian accent was imported, holding hints of American. She responded in Italian all the same.

"My brother is in love. He is very dear to me."

"Lucky man. He has found love and he has a sister as enchanting as you."

Heat blossomed in her cheeks as she smiled. As a rule, Ariabella kept her aura, the energy that all Olympians created, masked and guarded. One never knew anymore if the person next to them was a friend or foe. Her curiosity got the best of her, though. A sliver of her aura slipped past her shields, and with it, her power to recognize truth and lies.

His attraction was genuine. The emotion gave off a sweet energy that she could taste like fine chocolates. Finding people with true love had become a drug to her. Sensing their affections gave her a euphoric high.

"*Grazie.*" She pushed her wild blonde curls behind her ears. "You're not a native. I can hear it in your accent."

He cringed and shook his head. "Ouch. Is it that obvious?" He leaned in and spoke softly so no one else would hear him. "I've been working on my Italian for a long time."

Vero.

"It will suffice." Ariabella winked conspiratorially at him. She sipped her coffee and let her aura search over him…until she felt his Olympian aura, hiding just under the surface. Ariabella's back stiffened. What did she do now? He still sat back, quite relaxed, not aggressive at all, like he didn't notice her powers, nudging at his mind.

Maybe he was a half-breed? Maybe he didn't know he was Olympian? Maybe he knew and wasn't afraid of others of their kind? *Lucky him.*

"Where are you visiting from?" she asked, needing to feel him out before she turned her back on him and left.

"Originally, Montana. It gets far too cold for comfort in the winters. So I moved to Florida, found out I don't like the humidity and heat either." He scratched the short beard that framed nice lips and cordial smile. "Since I'm so picky, I thought I would travel the world and find somewhere that suits me."

"And you're giving Italy a try now?"

"*Si.*" He shrugged his shoulders and looked around at the outdoor café and took a deep breath of air. "It's perfect so far."

All he said was truth. What little of his aura she could feel didn't have the acidic bitterness of lies.

That was enough experimenting for one day. She withdrew her aura and gathered her things. "I hope you enjoy your stay. Will you be in town long?"

"Through the next semester, for sure. I'm taking architectural classes right around the corner at Waterloo." He set his book down on the table and held out a hand. "I'm Judah."

Not one to be impolite, she shuffled the flowers to the crook of her arm and took his hand. "Ariabella. Nice to meet you."

"Do you live around here?" He was quite handsome and his charming demeanor could easily distract her from the danger of outing herself as an Olympian.

"I do. In fact," she released his hand and picked up her bouquet, "I need to get back before the flowers wilt. I'm sure I'll see you around."

"I truly hope so." The kindness in his smile made her flush again. Judah ran his hands through his brown hair, moving the locks away from his eyes, kind brown eyes that held hers a second longer than she intended.

Ariabella nervously glanced away as her pulse quickened. "*Ciao.*"

He tipped an imaginary hat to her and resumed reading his book.

Ariabella couldn't help but grin when she glanced over her shoulder and caught him checking her out as she left. His shy wave made her sigh.

Yes, it was a glorious day indeed.

Judah pretended to read his book as the exquisite Ariabella walked away. She reminded him of a feather, floating away on a breeze, her long locks of golden hair wafting in the wind. Her feet barely touched the ground. Maybe she was actually a nymph? A fairy who danced around and spread magic wherever she went.

Whatever she was, she had his undivided attention—and not only because that was his assignment. Ariabella was so ravishing, it boggled his mind. He'd felt her aura searching him over and didn't hesitate to unlock enough of his own aura for her to know what he was. Her reaction hadn't escaped him. The way her shoulders went stiff and her nostrils flared might have been overlooked by someone who wasn't as intensely focused on her every movement.

On his way to Italy, he'd done research on Aletheians. Their power was also their downfall, depending on the strength of their gift. Some could merely sense the truth, but wouldn't know an outright lie. Some could determine lies, but could be fooled by half-truths. There were powerful Aletheians of old who could sense it all: truth, lies, lies of omission, and everything in between. From what he could tell from their encounter, she recognized his truths.

Judah *had* been raised in Montana and didn't like the cold. He *had* moved to Florida and didn't like the conditions there either, and he absolutely was a world traveler. He'd told her truths, no more than she needed to know.

Over the next couple of weeks, he tried to be in the places she frequented. One thing he had learned quickly at the onset of this mission: Ariabella didn't keep a steady schedule. Sometimes she stayed out late at the bar dancing and flirting, sometimes she was home by mid-afternoon and didn't leave her apartment. When she did work, which was only here and there, it was at a hole-in-the-wall bookstore. There, she would fill in from time to time for a few hours. If Judah was going to make any sort of connection with her, he was going to purposefully place himself in her path. The problem was figuring out said path.

If Ariabella didn't have any routines, he would have to find another way to insert himself into her life.

"Looks like I'm going to be doing a lot of reading," he said to himself, spying through binoculars from a distant rooftop as she danced into the bookstore, a gleaming smile on her face. He'd prepared a list of books that he could slowly inquire about in the store. In order to make sure it didn't appear too shady, he went in often, even if Ariabella wasn't working, so that the store owner would begin to expect him, and recognize and accept his presence as normal.

Judah did the same with the local businesses. He established his own routine so that people around would learn to overlook him walking down the same streets every day and eating the same meals at the same cafes often. Humans were creatures of habit and he made a point to blend in until shopkeepers knew him by name, waving as he passed by on his way to "class."

By doing this, he ran into Ariabella by accident a few times. His plan worked well, because after a month of being in town, she was so accustomed to his normalcy that she didn't hesitate to engage in small talk or wave.

It was exactly what he wanted.

It was exactly what killed him every time he saw that dazzling smile. Her unearthly beauty often knocked the breath out of his lungs. The feeling took him by surprise. Over his eighty-five years on this earth, he'd never been distracted from his mission. This time, however, his mission was his distraction. He watched over Ariabella all day long, until he knew she was asleep at night. Then he would sneak in his own rest.

He was supreme at spying, which was what got him this gig in the first place. And thank Zeus for that, because he didn't want to think of any other man watching her like he did.

One afternoon, he set out from his class to eat dinner and go home for the night. At least that was what it would look like to others. As he turned onto the street lining the Tiber, he saw the curtains of Ariabella's apartment waving in the wind. She only left the windows open if she was home. Purposefully and slowly, he sauntered down the street, a newspaper in one hand, water bottle in the other, whistling a tune she often hummed to herself.

"*Ciao*, Judah." She leaned out of her window and smiled down on him, an angel from the Heavens.

Holy Zeus, what a creation you've made.

"*Ciao*, Bella." He smiled in return, glad that on this mission, he didn't have to hide his attraction. In this case, it would only help.

"*Come va oggi?*" Her Italian was elegant and perfect, a language she turned into art. She turned a simple question like "how are you today" into poetry. He'd never loved the language more.

"Well, and you?" He shaded his eyes with the paper as he looked up.

"*Stupendamente.*" She pushed her long blonde hair off her shoulders. A gorgeous blush colored her cheeks every time she looked at him.

"It's a perfect afternoon for a stroll. Are you busy?" His heart hammered against his ribs as soon as the invitation was given. He hadn't asked because he was supposed to keep an eye out on her; he asked because he wanted to be in her presence—pure and simple.

Ariabella bit her bottom lip, her apprehension clear.

The tickle in his skull of her aura testing his honesty might have been an unwelcomed invasion for others; still, he allowed it, ignoring it so that she would think he was oblivious to her tests.

Instead, he thought about how her golden hair glittered in the sunlight and how her eyes sparkled with happiness all the time. His eyes followed the curve of her lips and he allowed his desire to taste them seep into his aura along with the deep longing to understand and court her. If she could see anything at all, she would see that he desired her—and that was a truth he couldn't hide, even if he wanted to.

With a deep breath, she nodded. *"Va bene. Si,* give me a moment?"

"Si, certo." Happiness bubbled up in his chest and he didn't bother to control it. He sat on a bench under the trees and waited for her to come downstairs.

It took a conscious effort to be himself and not mentally hide behind a persona. Instead of being afraid she would sense his true intentions, he allowed himself to fret over being liked as a potential boyfriend. Instead of worrying if she could read his physicals signs of deceit, he focused on showing his physical signs of attraction.

Yes, this would be the one job where he could allow his personal desires to overshadow his professional goals. He was a master chameleon; wouldn't be here if he wasn't. Not too many people could lie like he could. With Ariabella, however, it was in his best interest to be as honest as possible, a foreign concept.

When she stepped out of the building, her yellow sundress flowing about her knees and her lovely face lit with sunlight, he figured being honest about his intentions with Ariabella would be pretty damn easy. His mission was to keep her safe and happy. Making her happy would be his pleasure—and hopefully hers.

Ariabella sucked in a breath when Judah smiled at her and bent to kiss each cheek, as was customary. The woodsy scent of his cologne engulfed her senses and made her body hum with delight. Compared to her, he was such a large man; Thracian, if her suspicions were correct. He was quite tall and deliciously muscular. Not beefy or bulky, like the guys who lived at the gym; still, nicely rounded in the shoulders and chest.

"You look lovely today." His brown eyes, a couple shades darker than hers, scanned her from head to toe…twice. He extended his arm in a gentlemanly gesture.

"Thank you." She rested her hand in the crook of his elbow. "Did you have class?"

He groaned and nodded. "I want to explore the city, you know? Not be stuck in a classroom reading about it. The history is important and of course the original builders are interesting." He shrugged his wide shoulders. "I would simply rather *go*."

"Don't you and your friends go out? I've seen you around." Not that she'd been intentionally looking for him. When people walked the same streets every day, they were bound to run into each other. She didn't mind one bit. Judah was cute, sexy in a subtle, quiet way. Most of the men she attracted were boisterous and as wild as she was. They were firecrackers: dazzling in the moment, then gone with the breeze.

Judah seemed stable, grounded, an unfamiliar yet comfortable sensation. He set her at ease as they meandered down the sidewalk and chatted like old friends.

His voice was soft as he answered her various questions about himself and then asked his own about her. "I know you work in the bookstore occasionally. What else do you do?"

"I'd tell you, then I would have to kill you, and there's a lot of paperwork involved, so…" She acted very melodramatic about the whole bit.

Judah threw back his head, laughing. "I see, I see. For both our sakes, let's not go there, then."

After the caress of his laughter faded, she answered his question with her cover story. No one could know her real job. It was far too risky. Between Val D'Esta, the human police, and Rogues, there were spies everywhere. "I'm a forensic document examiner."

Judah's eyebrows went high in surprise. "You're kidding me?"

She shook her head. "I mainly analyze handwriting and signatures. You can tell a lot about a person by their handwriting. You can tell what mental state they are in depending on the brushstrokes, even what their basic personality is like."

"I don't mean to be insulting, but wasn't a lot of the handwriting analysis proven invalid in the 1980s?"

Slightly shocked yet impressed that he would know such a thing, Ariabella answered, "There were a lot of studies done on handwriting to base job performance and things of that nature. Most of them were invalid in that aspect. I mainly examine the validity of signatures on official documents, historic documents, and wills. I've studied the signatures of every diplomat, mafia boss, and celebrity who has ever signed an autograph."

"That's very impressive."

"I don't get called on too often, which is why I work in the bookstore occasionally. Even so, I've never been wrong." She lifted her chin, proud of her track record.

"Never?" His skepticism showed in the way he narrowed his eyes, even though he grinned. As they walked, the stores were closing for the night and the restaurants were preparing for the evening meal.

"I guess you could say I have a gift for these kinds of things." She risked the hint that she was different, hoping and praying he would catch it.

Judah nodded his head. "I have a strange feeling you're referring to more than women's intuition." He didn't look fully at her, instead giving her a side glance.

"I am."

They walked a few steps in silence before he took a deep breath and blew it out his mouth. "I…" He searched for the right word, tilting his head from side to side. "I *felt* you, the first time we met."

"Do you know why?" Ariabella angled her body so that no one else would hear their conversation. Her pulse kicked up and she realized he wasn't as ignorant as he let on.

Judah addressed the elephant head on. "I'm a Thracian. You're an Olympian. I felt your aura searching me. You've been hiding your aura from me. It's okay, though," he quickly assured her. "I understand."

Ariabella released the breath she'd been holding and his arm. She hugged herself. Now that their secrets were out on the table, what did she do? Apologize for searching his mind uninvited?

"I didn't mean to invade. A girl can't be too careful these days."

He waved her off. "You didn't see anything I didn't want you to." His cocky tone was followed by a huge grin. "We both know how to shield quite well. I was reading you too."

Ariabella's mouth hung open at his teasing. "Ah, *si*, smarty pants? And what did you see?"

"A kind woman who loves to dance and makes friends

everywhere she goes. You were trying to get away from me that day in the *caffé,* but you just *had* to stop and be polite. It was so cute."

Ariabella shivered with the truth in his words. He had read her like a book and she hadn't even known it. "I don't know if I should be impressed or frightened." She kept walking beside him, noting every street they took. This was her city, her neighborhood, and they were by no means alone. That didn't mean she was going to let her guard down.

Trust no one, her brother had said. Easy enough for everyone else around her—Judah, however, blurred the line.

Judah rubbed his heart. "Could you be impressed? It is much less offensive to my incredibly large male ego."

Ariabella giggled and nodded. They strolled up and down the stone streets until they reached one of her favorite places.

"Would you like to have dinner?" Judah shoved his hands in his pockets and rocked back on his heels. He nodded his head to the canopy that proudly displayed *Osteria.*

"Grazie, con piacere. My pleasure."

Judah pulled out her chair and seated her right under the white blooms of a potted jasmine. Lengthy meals at street cafes were second nature. They ate penne al'arrabiata and listened to the tourists attempt to speak horrible Italian to the waiters. They laughed and told stories about their travels. Judah had been all over the world and he was around her same age, young for Olympians, who lived to be hundreds, if not thousands, of years old. They sat at the tavern for hours, drinking and discussing everything from his studies of architecture to her hobby of photography. The more they drank, the more they talked. The more they talked, the more they drank until Ariabella's head was fuzzy and

Judah had to hold her hand as he paid the check and they ambled through the streets back to her place.

"Tell me about your gifts," Ariabella asked, unafraid to speak of their secret.

"I'm a Thracian. That is my gift." One side of his mouth kicked up. "I can hurt people very well." The wide, silly smile made her think otherwise.

"I'm aware you're Thracian. What is your gift? Even Thracians have been blessed with talents beyond fighting."

Judah was quiet for only a moment before he answered. "I have an eidetic memory. I remember everything after only seeing it once."

Half-truth. She might've been tipsy, but her powers still worked. At the moment, she didn't want to know if that was completely true or what it really meant. She wanted to flirt and play and seduce.

"Is that why you're taking classes in Italian architecture?" The alcohol had her head spilling. Mixed with her desire for Judah, she was flying high.

"I'm a lifelong student. And," he spread his arms wide to take in the scenery: the old multicolored buildings, the lush green vines that hung from the clothes lines and crept up the corners of the walls, "Who wouldn't want to come to Rome given the opportunity?"

"*Salute!*" Ariabella giggled, liquid giddiness coursing through her veins.

Judah chuckled at her as she danced about the narrow lanes and twirled in her dress. He caught her when she swirled right into his chest and threw her arms around his neck. They both stumbled to get their footing before laughing even harder. Judah leaned up against the old stone building and she stood between his legs. They held each other's eyes for a long moment while she relaxed against his firm body.

Judah was smart and so cute. *Santo Zeus!* His kind eyes and sweet smile seduced her easily. He wasn't her type, not really. Usually, her flames were the pretty men that ended up on Italian fashion magazines. They attracted attention and were often the life of the party. Their trysts usually ended because people naturally gravitated to Ariabella, and a lesser man couldn't be upstaged.

Not Judah. Even for a Thracian, he was quiet and calm. He didn't mind that waiters flirted with her or that she flirted back. He didn't seem to care that men ogled her while she ate and stared while she walked down the streets. Nothing triggered jealousy in his aura or his actions. She liked that. It felt freeing.

Ariabella rubbed her fingertips against the scruff of his short beard, watching him lick his lips. Her entire body flushed at the thought of tasting those lips and having him taste her in return. She cleared her throat. "I have to help at the bookstore tomorrow, but I would like to see you again tomorrow night."

"I would like that too." His voice had gone husky, his eyes too, lingering on her lips. "I want to kiss you, Bella."

"Don't waste a perfect opportunity." She smiled and tiptoed up so he didn't have to bend down so far.

His lips met hers with a feather-soft touch and lightning sprang into her veins, buzzing through her entire body with fiery electricity.

She gasped and pulled away. "What was that?"

Judah stared down at her with wide eyes and a slack jaw. "I don't know. Let's do it again." With one hand wrapping around her waist to pull her closer, he buried his other hand in her velvet hair and took her mouth with passion.

Ariabella's eyes drifted closed on a sigh, her chest tightened, her breasts suddenly swelled. Desire sprang up from a well so deep within, she couldn't understand where it had been all her life. She ran her hands over his firm chest and up his neck, holding on tightly. Judah moaned and pulled her tighter against his hard body. She clenched her thighs together, afraid she would come undone right there on the street. *Santo cielo,* he tasted like pure sex. Images of him naked and hovering over her body flashed in her head, so vivid it was like a memory. Was there more to this adorable man than he was letting on? Was he some sort of Olympian seducer?

Ariabella pushed away, her chest heaving with every panting breath. "What have you done to me?"

Judah had the same reaction she did. Each breath was labored, as though he'd run a marathon. He shifted his legs and Ariabella noticed the bulge in his jeans. He stared at her with an open infatuation so intense, his eyes were on fire from within. "I should ask you the same thing."

In all her years, she'd never experienced a kiss that felt like a brand. Olympian magic was a strange thing and she couldn't begin to understand its intricacies. Was this magic? Was it lust? Was it real or was Judah playing her somehow? As much as she hated to, she had to discover the truth.

"Judah," she met his eyes and let her aura wash over him, probing his mind, "tell me the truth." With those four words, she captured him in a spell he couldn't break. Face-to-face, no one could resist her commands.

Judah blinked a couple times. He was still aware of everything; he simply was forced to answer in truth.

How she phrased her questions was key. She didn't want to abuse her power, but her brother had told her to be careful, after all. "Did you manipulate me to desire you?"

"No." Judah's brows dipped as if he couldn't believe she would think such a thing.

"Are you using your Thracian gifts on me somehow?"

"Of course not."

"Have you done something to force my affections in any way?"

Judah nodded his head and cupped her cheeks with his hands. "Yes. I've tried desperately to see you as much as possible without it being obvious and I'm trying my best to impress you tonight."

"So you do like me?"

"Very much."

Guilt settled in her chest and she closed her eyes, retracted her aura, and freed Judah from the compulsion.

He blinked away the spell and his eyes focused on her again. "What—why did you do that?"

"*Perdonami!* I'm sorry." Ariabella stepped back, out of his arms, and fisted her hands at her side, preparing for the anger that would surely follow. "I had to know if you were doing something to make me want you."

Judah took a deep breath and narrowed his eyes. "So *that* is your true Olympian gift? You're Aletheian, a truth seeker." He huffed out a breath and shook his head. His jaw tensed up as he cast his eyes away from her.

Ariabella nodded, keeping her face down. Shame washed over her in waves.

He rubbed the bridge of his nose. "Just because you force your gifts on others, doesn't mean we all do." The hurt and heat of his anger in his aura brushed against her.

She gasped at the harshness of his tone; it made her sick with guilt. *What have I done?*

"Next time, ask me. I would've happily told you the truth."

She crossed her arms over her chest and rubbed her bare shoulders. "And that is?"

"That I've wanted to know you from the moment I saw your face, that everything you do turns me on, that being with you tonight has been perfect, and yeah, that spark between us is real."

Ariabella swallowed hard and clenched her eyes closed, fighting tears. What had she done? "I'm sorry. I was scared. My brother called me not too long ago and told me to be careful, not to trust anyone and I—" She shook her head quickly. "—I assumed something this exceptional couldn't be real, that you had to have done something."

"Like I said, next time, just ask me, Bella. I don't have a problem telling you how much I want you." He stepped forward and put a hand around the nape of her neck and placed a kiss on her forehead. "I'll see you around." She had been so lost in him, she hadn't noticed they were outside her building.

"Judah?" she called to him. "Please forgive me. I'm sorry."

"As am I," he called over his shoulder, not even bothering to turn around.

Ariabella went upstairs alone and locked herself in her apartment, leaning her back against her door. *Perche?* Why did she have to be *so* stupid? Judah had been a perfect gentleman all night. They'd laughed, talked, gotten to know each other, and it had all been so wonderful. Of course, she had to be paranoid and mess it all up.

Needing to talk to someone, she picked up the phone and called Bridget, her closest sister. Unlike when she called her brother, she could speak her native tongue.

"Hey! I'm so glad you called. I'm off work this weekend. Want to do something?"

"Please." Ariabella closed her eyes, the comfort of family instantly warming her. "Do you have a moment? I need to talk."

"Of course. What's wrong? I can hear it in your voice."

Ariabella smiled. That was exactly what she'd said when Dante called. Despite the distance, their family remained connected and that meant everything to her. "I think I ruined my chances with one of the most incredible men I've ever met."

"Wait, you're upset over a man?" Bridget was truly dumbfounded. "You *never* get upset over men. He must be something special."

Ariabella told Bridget all about Judah, from the moment they met to their fantastic night together and what she'd done to ruin it.

Bridget sighed. "How many times have I told you that people don't like their minds being invaded, Aria? Your gift can be terrifying. People need their secrets, their privacy. Our thoughts are all we truly own in this world."

Ariabella fell back on her bed and looked at the night sky out her open window. "I can't help it. He was so…*intense*, so incredible, and I foolishly assumed it couldn't be real. I've never shied away from basic attractions, you know that. Judah is…I've never had anything…this, this, I don't know, I don't even know the word."

Bridget chuckled on the other end of the phone, her laugh a copy of her sister's. "Wow, a man who renders you speechless. That's one for the history books. Did you ever think that perhaps the gods sent him to you?"

"If the gods sent him, I've spit on their gift. He may never speak to me again and I do *not* blame him. I'm such a fool. It has only been minutes since we parted and I already miss his company, Bridget. How crazy does that sound?" She scrubbed a hand over her face and padded over to the window, praying that by some miracle Judah would be walking by, knowing he wouldn't be.

"Pretty romantic, actually." Bridget swooned. "I'd give anything for that kind of desire for a man. Why can't the gods send me a Judah?" She laughed.

"I'm the eldest, brat. Wait your turn."

"Well, stop pissing them off. I want babies before I'm one hundred." Bridget teased her all the time. There was nothing as precious—or blunt—as a sister. The girls made plans for Bridget to come to Trastevere for the weekend, since Ariabella had gone to her home in Ancona for their last visit a few weeks ago. Ariabella sat on her balcony for a long time, sipping a glass of wine and wondering what she was going to do about Judah. If the gods gave her a second chance, she wouldn't screw it up again.

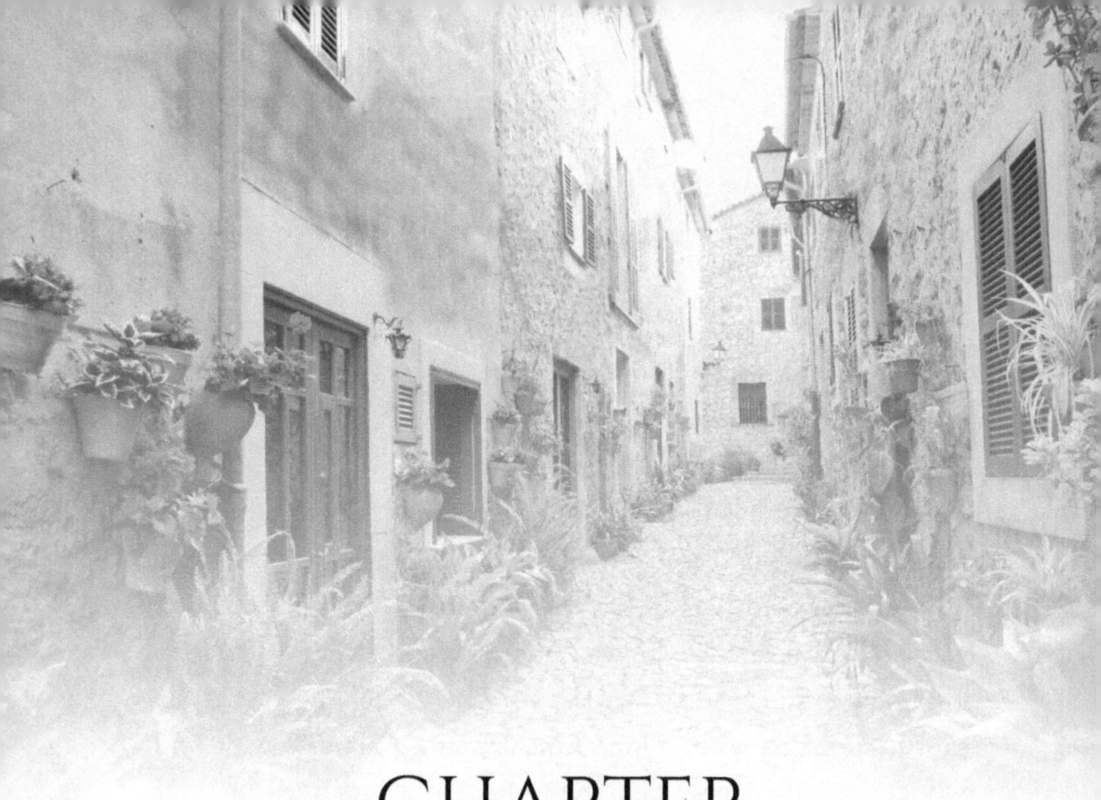

CHAPTER THREE

As soon as he rounded the corner, out of her sight, Judah slipped up to the roof of her building. He carefully padded over the eaves until he was right above her window and sat down. He was silent as death and blended in with the blackness.

Tonight had *not* ended the way he had hoped. He rubbed the bridge of his nose. Man, if she'd asked the right questions, he would've been busted in a second. He had let his guard down, been enjoying the wine and the high that was Ariabella, and nearly screwed up.

Her kiss still tingled on his lips. The floral scent of her perfume lingered on his shirt. Judah fisted his hands. *Damn.* That kiss stamped her mark on him, lighting a spark in his soul that he couldn't anticipate. Where did it come from? What did it mean?

The use of her powers wasn't what angered him. After all, he was the one spying on her day and night. He knew every move she made and every phone call she received. If anyone was guilty of abusing power, it was him—and it ate at him like a disease, especially now.

She didn't know his sins against her and his superior officer didn't know his personal feelings towards her. It was probably best that he walked away when he did.

He had to react in a logical manner. Under normal circumstances, an Olympian would be outraged at the hypnotism she performed. The forceful use of powers was a violation of basic rules and considered quite rude in most countries. If he read her correctly, her aura had held fear over her strong attraction. That fear won over the guilt of forcing his answers.

His cell phone vibrated, his app indicating that Ariabella was making a call. He recognized the phone number she dialed as her sister's. There was a moment when his duty to keep an eye on her battled with his need to know what she said about him. It was an invasion either way. He would rather know he was following orders…not merely hoping she talked to her sister about him.

Instead of tapping in to the phone call, he listened to her talking through her window.

I think I ruined my chances with one of the most incredible men I've ever met…

Judah let out a deep breath in relief. She did like him. He listened as Ariabella described their interactions over the last couple weeks. She, too, had been attracted to him since the first time they'd met.

I can't help it. He was so…intense, so incredible, and I foolishly assumed it couldn't be real. I've never shied away from basic attractions, you know that. Judah is...I've never had anything...this, this, I don't know, I don't even know the word.

He understood her inability to label what had happened between them. The entire night had been magical. Ariabella was full of life and joy, turning the unremarkable into something magnificent. He hadn't thought twice about relaxing, having a beer, laughing like he hadn't done in years. If he could only hold on to that feeling for the rest of his life.

If the gods sent him, I've spit on their gift. He may never speak to me again and I do not blame him. I'm such a fool. It has only been minutes since we parted and I already miss his company, Bridget. How crazy does that sound?

Air rushed out of his lungs and pinched his eyes closed. He hugged his knees and rested his chin on them, overlooking the river and the city beyond. Judah would definitely speak to her again—and not because it was his duty. Any woman who tangled him up as fast as she did was worth second, third, or fourth chances.

A couple days later, he entered the bookstore with a bouquet of flowers. He intentionally shielded his aura so she wouldn't feel him coming. The smell of leather, paper, and fresh morning air filled the long, skinny store. Ariabella stood on a stool, stretching her arm up to put a book on a tall shelf. She was such a tiny thing, barely over five feet.

"I'll be right with you," she said as she struggled to push the tome back into place.

Judah came up beside her, easily reaching the book to help her push it back. "Allow me." His hand grazed over hers and electricity sparked between them.

Large, innocent brown eyes met his with surprise. "Judah."

The way she whispered his name made his chest ache. With the help of the stool, she was at eye level. *"Ciao."* Her chest heaved up and down with every breath.

He swallowed hard, not needing to fake his nervousness in the slightest. "I hope it's okay that I'm here. I needed to see you again."

Pink traveled up her neck and into her cheeks. "I'm glad."

Judah extended a hand to help her off the stool. She never broke eye contact as she stepped down.

He presented the flowers. "For you."

Ariabella smiled wide, her perfect white teeth gleaming, so radiant it broke his heart. "Thank you." She lifted them to her face and closed her eyes as she inhaled their scent. "Mmm." Brown eyes flickered to his, then darted away. "I don't deserve these."

"Every woman deserves flowers."

She ducked behind a wall to fetch a glass of water to hold the flowers and Judah took the moment to search the titles for something that piqued his interest. A moment later, she emerged with the flowers and sat them right by the register for all to see.

"I've been thinking," he said, leaning over the counter that separated them.

"Me too." She played with her fingernails and bit her bottom lip. "I'm so sorry, Judah. I insulted you, I know that."

"That's not what I was thinking about." Judah grazed her fidgeting fingers with his own. "I was thinking about your smile and how your eyes shine when you talk to people. I've been thinking—dreaming, actually—about that kiss."

Ariabella's blush was beginning to take the number one spot on his list of favorite sights in the world. "Yeah?"

"Yeah." He glanced around the store to make sure they were alone. "I can hardly concentrate on anything else."

Air whooshed from her lips as she released the breath she held. "Nor can I."

"You said something that worried me, about your brother telling you not to trust people?"

The change in her was minute, yet instant. She stood straighter, no longer leaning forward intimately. Her nostrils flared and her fingers retreated from his touch. "I said that?" Ariabella busied herself by picking up a stack of magazines and brushing past him to go place them on the racks by the front door.

"I thought you were all about the truth?"

She shrugged it off. "My brother is protective. He's looking out for me. All brothers do that."

A couple of people came into the store and she forced a smile, asking if she could help them find something. Judah was patient. He stood out of the way and let her do her job until they purchased a couple books and left.

"Bella." Judah touched her elbow when she tried to walk past him. "Please, talk to me."

"Not here." She smiled again at a new customer. "Meet me in the Piazza di Santa Maria this evening."

Judah nodded. "I get out of class around six. It's right around the corner." He brought her knuckles up to his lips. Again, the spark between them was practically visible. It tugged at his heart, making him regret all the secrets he must keep from her, making him wish he could tell her everything and give her the truth she so desired. By all the gods, he was slowly falling for this woman and he shouldn't.

Ariabella touched his cheek. "I'll see you tonight. Thanks for the flowers."

Judah left her to work and he went back to his place. As he entered his apartment, his cell phone jingled with a text message.

Report.

He typed back his response. *No change.* That was all his superior officer needed. He trusted Judah to handle any situation and to stay the course.

Thank the gods his superior officer didn't know how he was falling for the mark. Sexual interactions with the subject of the mission were not necessarily forbidden. Many trained spies slept with their targets in order to procure information during pillow talk.

If he slept with Ariabella, it would be because he was crazy about her and she willingly invited him into her bed. Some Thracians might use sex against women, but Judah would never stoop that low, especially not with the fascinating woman who waited for him to get out of class.

He set down his backpack, full of books he'd read once and never cracked again, beside the table where she waited. "Hey."

A guarded smile greeted him and it hurt his heart. "Hey." Her delicate fingers wrapped around a mug of coffee, so he ordered the same, though he didn't want it.

There was no wasting time; she dove right in to the conversation. "My brother called me about a month ago, telling me that weird things were happening in our world. He was adamant that I be careful about who I come in contact with."

"Why?" Judah accepted his coffee and resisted the urge to take her by the hand. Instead, he gripped his mug like she did.

"I don't know. His warnings don't seem to apply to you. That's what matters. I really like you, Judah. I didn't mean to force your answers."

"Of course you meant to. That's why you did it." There was no accusation in his tone, nothing bitter or angry in his aura. Only a simple honesty that left her feeling shameful.

"I panicked. My gift is the only defense I have. I'm not a trained Thracian. I don't have offensive skills." She pushed her hair behind her ears. "The truth has kept me safe my entire life." Her soft, high voice was barely a whisper. "It's second nature to seek it when I have doubts."

"I accept your apology, even though you're avoiding the subject. Are you in danger?" Judah gave in to his primal urges and laced his fingers through hers. "I can protect you, Bella."

"I know you can." The corners of her mouth turned up. "I'm not sure what my brother meant. I don't know if I'm in danger; at least, he hasn't said anything specific. What I do know is that every time I see you, something inside me gravitates to you the way the Tiber seeks the sea. I've never felt that before. I barely know you." She laughed at the absurdity of it, moisture gathering in her eyes. "I was scared I blew it."

"You didn't blow it. It's no different for me. The gods often surprise us when we least expect it." He reached up and swept a strand of hair from her cheek. "So what do we do?"

Ariabella leaned in and he mirrored her posture. "How about we start with dinner and see where it goes from there?"

Joy sang in his veins when she blessed him with one of her dazzling smiles. Like the night before, they laughed and talked for hours until the sun went down and the streetlights came on. When they grew tired of sitting, Judah took her by the hand and they walked down the streets in an aimless trail. It didn't matter where they went, as long as they went together.

Once again, she was in a short, flowy dress and he couldn't keep his eyes off her. Ariabella was pure sunshine even in the middle of the night. She glowed with happiness and warmth. Everyone knew her, everyone seemed to adore her, and she returned their affections. If one person could embody light, it was her.

Judah's hands zinged with every touch, every brush of their bodies as they walked. Being with her made him hold his head a bit higher, made him smile more, and worry less. He didn't have to pretend to be happy or content or interested in every nuance—and how long had his existence depended on his ability to pretend? As long as he could remember. He was so well-versed at faking it, he'd almost forgotten how to be real.

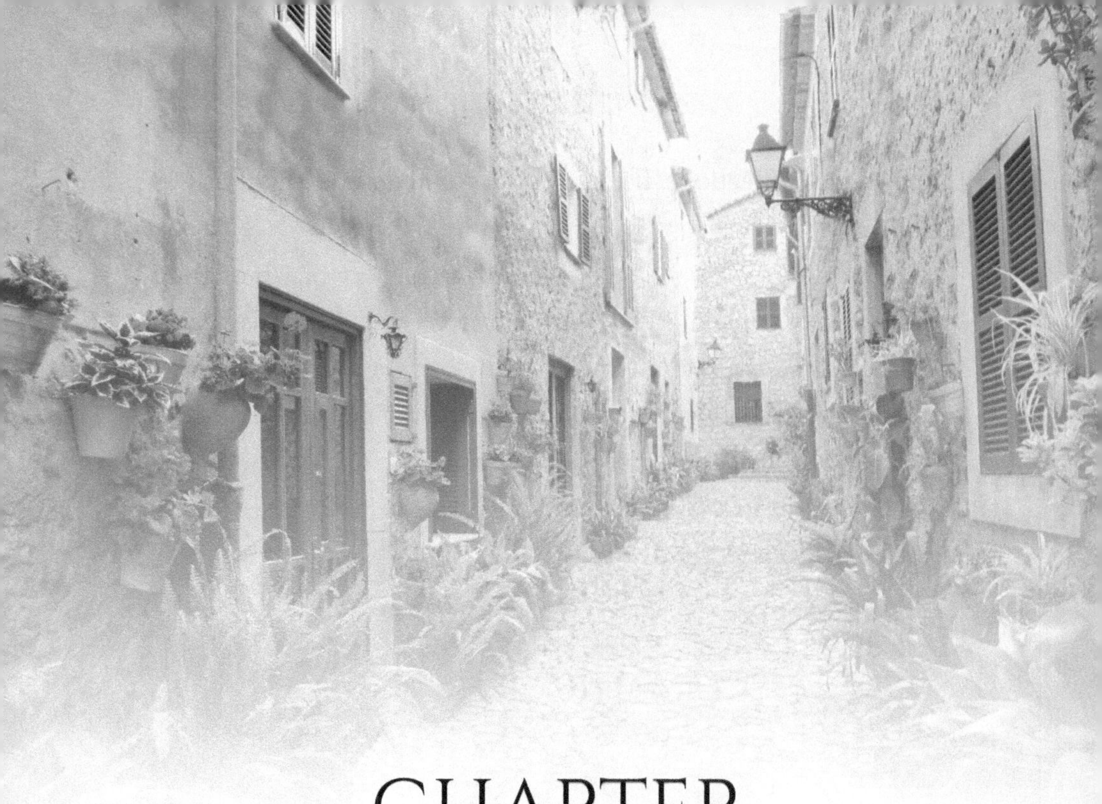

CHAPTER FOUR

OVER THE NEXT WEEKS, SWEET ARIABELLA BROUGHT HIM BACK to life after long being buried in a grave of his own making. She unearthed a piece of him each time they were together. It was against the rules, what he was doing. There was no following a script or sticking to a persona or a character he was playing. He wasn't undercover in the sense that he had to keep his opinions or true feelings to himself.

He had the pleasure one weekend of meeting her younger sister, Bridget, who was shockingly opposite of what he expected. Where Ariabella was petite, blonde, and fairy-like, Bridget was tall, dark-headed, and had the willowy grace of a ballerina. Their faces held similarities. Both women had brown eyes, straight, thin noses, and gorgeous wide smiles.

"Do you have a brother?" Bridget asked after dinner, making Judah grin as he shook his head. "A cousin, maybe?" She made a clicking noise in her mouth when he shook his head again. "Damn the luck."

"Tell us about the Thracians," Ariabella asked him over dinner that night. "What's it like, being right there in the same Haven as Master Ryse Castille? He scares the hell out of me."

Speaking of names that made people shiver. "Master Ryse is…" What was the right word for the Master Thracian? One adjective couldn't handle Ryse Castille. Judah blew out a breath, allowing his cheeks to balloon out. "Ryse Castille is power incarnate."

He had their rapt attention. They were hungry for information and he fed them. "When Ryse enters the Haven, the whole Haven seems to instantly fill with his aura. As his students, we always knew when he'd returned from the human realm. If he stepped foot in a classroom, he owned it. Even the Elites, the most hardened, honed Thracian warriors, submit to him and that spoke volumes to me." He took a drink of wine. The girls were quiet, still needing more.

"The thing about Ryse is that he truly cares about our people. We never questioned his loyalty to the gods. Training us wasn't left to his minions. No, Ryse was in the pits, sparring with us. He was in the classroom teaching the laws, the ethics, the great responsibility of being a Thracian.

"Prince Hayden was right with his brother, teaching. Hayden is incredibly smart…and deceptively dangerous. People assume that he is more brains than brawn. They forget his older brother is the Master Thracian."

"And Ryse trained him too?" Bridget said, captivated. "Though he's not Thracian?"

Judah nodded. "Oh yes. Living in the same household as Master Ryse has its advantages."

Bridget sighed. "Prince Hayden is so cute. Now you tell me he's smart and knows how to protect a woman? I'm in love!"

Ariabella giggled. "I thought you were in love with Prince Ashton? Wasn't he the Prince Charming you've always wanted?"

Blushing, Bridget leaned in and whispered to Judah, "I used to have posters of him all over my bedroom."

Judah didn't want to ruin the mood by pointing out that Ashton's little sister, Salina, was the person who murdered Master Ryse's mate. These girls were not raised in America. They were raised in a country where the Avondales reigned supreme. Where their Deities were modern and sophisticated, and revered like movie stars. The Avondales fit in the human world. They amassed fortunes, lived in mansions, owned vacation homes all over the globe, drove the most expensive cars, owned yachts and casinos, and lived their lives right out in the open. The European Olympians loved them for it.

The American Deities, like most others, were not meshed with human society. They held fast to the old traditions and ways of the gods. They lived in the safety of the Havens, in their ancient castles, not relying on money but talents to get what they needed. The Castilles, while still having the wealth needed to rule in the human world, didn't obtain ostentatious cars or mansions. Their fingerprint in the human world was virtually nonexistent. Yet they thrived as the most powerful of all the Deities. And the American Olympians loved them for it.

Judah settled on toasting to all the Deities to keep the mood light and happy. The time would come when they had to talk about the tragedies of their people. Tonight was not that time.

The two girls shared stories, told tales on each other, and the three of them laughed until the early morning hours. Saturday was a flurry of shopping and exploring some of the places the tourists wouldn't know about. As much as he'd researched things about the city, he couldn't have found these tips online. Bridget knew of a woman who was a Paean and massage therapist. She used her powers and aura to relax the body in a way a human never could. Ariabella took them to a private market where certain foods were grown by Earth Elementalists. The produce was so delicious and perfect, it blew his mind. He bit into a tomato that was as delicious as an apple and just as satisfying.

Bridget and Ariabella giggled when it dripped down his chin. Judah didn't mind laughing at himself, not if it meant entertaining the girls.

They dropped off the food at Ariabella's place and Bridget flopped down on the couch. "You know what we should do tonight? We should go dancing. Do you dance, Judah?"

"The more I drink, the better I get." It was one of the many things he had to learn for his line of work. Women were more receptive to men who danced well. His lessons had served their purpose over the years.

The thought of grinding against Ariabella to a sexy thump of bass sounded too delectable to pass up. Especially when she winked at him with a seductive grin on her face. "I'll have to change into something suitable."

"I like what you have on now." Judah put an arm around her waist and spun her about the kitchen. "See, it twirls."

Ariabella's eyes sparkled. She insisted that they meet up later at a local tavern for drinks. He kissed her cheek and left, excited to see what their night would hold.

Later, dressed in his nicest clothes, Judah waited outside the tavern. It was closer to his apartment than Ariabella's, so he decided to meet them there.

His mouth dropped open when he saw Ariabella walking down the street towards him. The little pixie had transformed into a vixen.

Air left her lungs when she noticed Judah leaned against the building, one knee lifted with his foot braced up. He straightened when she approached, his eyes widening and his jaw going slack. Heat bubbled up in her belly at the way his eyes traveled up and down her body, caressing each curve.

Bridget had helped pin her hair up and do her makeup, one of the perks of having a fashionista sister. Her eyes were dark with shadow and the red of her lips matched the red, silky blouse that dipped deep between her breasts, showing off her modest chest. A silver chain around her midriff tickled her stomach as she walked. Tight, black leather pants hung low on her hips, showing off a few inches of her skin. She felt sexy and his reaction only added to her confidence.

"Roll up your tongue, Judah," Bridget teased and she patted his cheek.

That cheek instantly turned red. "I'm not sure I can." He spoke as if he was under a spell. He took a deep breath and his Adam's apple bobbed up and down when he swallowed. "Wow."

Ariabella also had to get her breathing under control. Judah was in a black button-up and olive-colored slacks. He smelled fresh and clean, delicious. His dark brown eyes met hers and held them as a smile grew on his face. She couldn't look away. The world disappeared around them and all that mattered was Judah.

"You look…wow." He ran his hand through his hair.

Ariabella smiled so hard, it almost hurt her cheeks. "You said that already."

"It's the best I can come up with." He chuckled nervously.

"It's perfect," she said and sighed.

Bridget cleared her throat and suppressed her grin. "Excuse me, lovebirds, I'd like to go pick up a man, and they are all *inside* the bar." She thumbed towards the door. "Shall we?"

Judah wrapped an arm around Ariabella's waist and pulled her to his side. "I'm keeping you close."

His hand on her bare skin sent flames to her belly and lower.

The alcohol flowed, the music thumped, and Ariabella gave in to the beat. After a few drinks, she pulled Judah up to dance and Bridget found herself a partner.

It turned sensual quickly as she brushed her body against the firmness of Judah's. She delighted in the way his hands held her hips and found their way down to cup her bottom. He could move in a way that made her want to purr. He also knew how to have fun and be silly, which was equally sexy.

They held each other tight during a slow song, and she tiptoed up to whisper in his ear. "Will you come home with me tonight?"

A gravelly, deep rumble emanated from his chest and his arm tightened around her. He bent his face down into the curve of her neck and kissed his way up to her ear. Chills ran over her body, even though she was burning up.

"I don't know if you can handle that." His lips grazed over her ear and she shivered.

Red hot desire pulsed between her legs. "Why?"

"Because I'll take you to bed and I'll fall in love with you. That's not safe for either of us."

Ariabella's eyes flickered up to his, her body missing a beat. "Judah." She gripped his neck, resisting the urge to use her gifts to see into his mind. His words tasted of truth, like pure water with a hint of cool peppermint. Underneath, the truth ran an undercurrent of affection and lust that made her toes curl. "What the bloody hell is the pull between us?"

He shook his head, running his hands over her back. "I have no idea. Damn, it's strong, Bella."

She closed her eyes and breathed in the comfort of his aura, the sweet-smelling scent of his endearment. "Do the gods anoint Thracians and their mates? Is that possible?" Her brown eyes fluttered open and she met his stare.

"I… I don't know. Not many Thracians are lucky enough to find love, much less a mate."

There was no containing the joy that spread across her face and through her body. "Are we really talking about this? After we've only known each other for such a short time?"

"If the gods can create a Divine Grace perfectly suited for a Deity and give them the ability to love each other the moment they meet, surely they can bless us with something fractionally less potent yet just as permanent." Judah grinned and nuzzled his nose to hers. "I've never been drawn to anyone the way I'm drawn to you, Bella. When I'm apart from you, there's this pressure in my chest—"

Ariabella rubbed at her sternum, knowing exactly what he meant. "Like you can't take a full breath."

"Exactly." He cupped her cheek. "As if you're my oxygen." Dipping his head further, he brushed a kiss across her lips and sparks flew. Fingers bunched up the fabric of her blouse and he pulled her closer.

She feathered her hands through his soft brown hair and gripped it, deepening their kiss. The velvet warmth of his tongue slid across her lips and she welcomed him in. Molten hot desire coursed from head to toe and stole her breath.

"We have to get out of here," she panted against his lips.

"Your sister?"

"Is a big girl and knows her way home. Trust me, it would take a hardy man to take her down." They glanced over at Bridget and waved goodbye when she finally looked up from the cute guy she was flirting with. Bridget wiggled her brows and blew them a kiss, waving for them to go ahead and leave.

Her sister could turn air unto bullets if necessary. She didn't need Ariabella's protection. At that moment, all Ariabella wanted was to get her hands on Judah.

The two of them hurriedly walked to her place, stopping in alleyways and kissing until the passion and aching need was unbearable. By the time she opened the lock on her apartment, Judah had her pants unbuttoned and she tore at his shirt.

Desire was a writhing beast within her skin, screaming to be sated. Her mouth devoured his, licking and biting, ramping up his reactions. Judah had her naked in record time, throwing her clothing as he peeled it from her body.

She giggled when he almost tripped as he kicked off his shoes and dropped his pants. Seeing his playful smile melted her insides and reminded her it wasn't only his body that she wanted—it was his heart.

"Come here, little minx." Judah's strong arms lifted her right off the ground and she wrapped her legs around his waist, grinding her wet core into his erection. A deep growl came from his chest and he gripped her bottom with both hands.

"Take me, Thracian. Show me how a warrior claims his

woman." Her heart beat so fast, it felt like a drumroll sounding off in her chest.

Challenge accepted; Judah didn't waste time with foreplay. They fell on the bed, kissing and groping, needing one another. She was hot and ready, simmering and aching for him. He spread her legs and hovered over her body, hesitating only for a second before propelling into her so deep, she bowed up off the bed and gasped, letting out a stream of curses.

Santo cielo, he felt good inside her; strong, hard, and hot. When his eyes met hers and she saw the mutual pleasure on his face, she knew this was something different, something special.

⚹

Judah's vision went blurry when he drove into Ariabella. Her tiny body gripped him like a vise and made him see stars. Hearing his pixie, with her high, soft voice, cursing like a sailor in several languages, made him grin with satisfaction.

"Does that *claim* you enough?" he teased her, running his hand up her thigh to massage her bottom and bury himself even deeper between her legs.

"Mission achieved," she panted.

"Oh, baby, I'm just getting started."

Ariabella's eyes rolled back in her head when he started to move and set the pace. Her creamy skin took on a pink blush and she moaned with every beat of his rhythm. *Great gods of Olympia.* Their bodies moved together in perfect sync, meeting and parting like waves dancing on the shoreline. With every eager kiss, he could taste her delight.

If only he could press the pause button on this moment and capture it to hold forever. Such beauty, such passion, such perfection.

To think, he never knew she existed before two months ago. He'd been missing a piece of his soul for so long and didn't realize it until he met Ariabella. What if he had never received the call? What if he hadn't been on leave when it came through? What if someone else had been assigned to protect her? He would've missed out on a world of happiness.

Judah didn't waste a moment of their time together. He took her in every position he could think of, pinning her down with his body, lying underneath her while she writhed on top of him, her modest breasts bouncing in temptation. Not an inch of her skin went untouched or unloved. By the time they were done, he wanted to own her inside and out. He wanted to memorize the curves of her ass, the smell of her shampoo, the taste of her heated skin, and the sounds of her exertion.

If this was to be his mate, he wanted to learn everything about her.

Later, in the shadows of the night, he held her to his chest and tried to calm his raging pulse. Now that he knew what love felt like, he wanted it "forever."

He said the word out loud, testing it on his tongue.

"Hmm?" A sleepy, sated Ariabella leaned up to see what he'd said.

"I, um, can we have this forever? Can I have *you* forever?" He ran his hands through her golden hair, loving the fact that she was exhausted and sweaty from their sex. As his American friends would say, she had been ridden hard and put up wet.

More than anything, he loved the dazed, happy gleam in her eyes and the silly grin on her face. Who knew such delicacies existed for mortal men?

"How can I say no to an offer like that?" Such sweetness in her voice made his body melt once again. "Are you sure, Judah?"

"You're the one who can drag the truth of me." He laughed. "Do it."

She crawled up his chest to kiss him once more. "I don't have to. I can hear it in your words."

"I'm the one taking the risk. I can't tell what you're thinking or if you—"

Ariabella put a finger over his lips. "Did me screaming out your name like a banshee not give you a clue?"

Judah shivered. She was so full of passion, so full of life and light.

"I bet we woke the neighbors. I don't think I have *ever* yelled out during sex before." She giggled and bit her bottom lip. Her cheeks were still red from earlier and she glowed. "You're not like any man I've ever met. You make me feel safe, even though we're jumping off a cliff."

Victory rang out like cathedral bells. He leaned up on his elbow and faced her. "Let's jump," he said excitedly. "Let's go for it."

Ariabella lay on her belly and faced him. "I have to tell you, Judah, I've never been in a long-term relationship." She rolled her eyes. "Not like humans think of long term, rather like Olympians. My longest relationship was ten years and we only saw one another a handful of times a month. That's nothing in terms of mating material."

He shrugged one shoulder. "What does that matter? Neither have I. Then again, I've never *wanted* to be mated to anyone before. I guess I've been waiting for you."

Her smile was the greatest gift he'd ever received.

"I'm willing to try, if you are." She nibbled that bottom lip again, her eyes searching his for the truth, even though her aura remained retracted. That had to have been hard for her, a woman used to relying on her gods-given gifts to make such decisions. She simply trusted him at his word.

Guilt settled in his gut. He had to adjust his mission tactics if he was to be honest with his lover and still obey his mission operator. No more spying. No more eavesdropping on her phone calls, nothing invasive. If he needed to protect her, he would do it like every husband protects his wife—by being there for her and communicating with her. If his officer had a problem with that, he would deal with it. This was his woman and he couldn't hurt her.

The sun woke Judah up that morning. An angel lay in the bed beside him, her bare body sprawled across him and his hand on her ass. *Holy Zeus*, she was so divine.

He had to make things right. He had to let her know why he was truly in Trastevere.

Judah wiggled out from under her, glad that he'd worn her out once again only a few hours prior. Ariabella was out cold. He slipped on his pants and padded to the kitchen to find Bridget sprawled out on the couch. As hard as he tried not to, he ended up waking her when he dropped a plastic cup on the floor.

"Morning, cutie." Bridget grinned and stretched. "I hope you took care of my sister last night."

Wow, awkward.

"Um, I, yeah." Judah laughed nervously and poured himself some orange juice. "Sorry we left you—"

"Don't be." Bridget waved him off. "I had fun and I know my way around."

"Good." He sipped the juice.

"Besides, I met someone who knows you. He was totally hot, all dark and mysterious. Um, Martin, Mark, Max, yeah, Max, no,

Maxim, that's it. Maxim." She yawned out the string of names like it was no big deal. "Short black hair, lots of tattoos."

Judah's blood ran cold.

"He said he knew you. I'd bet money he was Thracian, even though he was shielding his aura incredibly well."

As not to frighten Bridget about the monster under her bed, he swirled the juice around in the glass and played it off. "Yeah, yeah. I know him. Hope he was nice to you. I'd hate to have to kick his ass, you know?" Judah grinned. All the while, fear iced over his veins. If only Bridget had known that she'd danced with death last night. Gods help him, the thought of something happening to one of the girls because of him…

Maxim the Magician was in Trastevere. A man whose loyalties and activities were questionable at best had made contact with his beloved's sister. What in the name of the gods was Maxim doing in this city?

Bridget let out a sigh and snuggled into the couch, clearly not ready to get up. "He was nice. He said to tell you hello." She fell right back to sleep as quickly as she'd awakened.

Judah rinsed out his cup and went back to Ariabella. He stood right inside the door of the bedroom, taken aback by how much he cared for her and how scared he was that Maxim was in the area and he hadn't known it. The sneakiness of it didn't settle right, how Maxim had spoken to Bridget, an innocent woman, not him, a fellow Thracian. What game was he trying to play?

If Ariabella was in danger, Maxim could very well be the cause of it. He knew Judah was here and baited him with Bridget. There was no doubt where Maxim was at this moment and Judah needed to meet him before he came to Ariabella's home.

He slid into bed and gently tried to wake Ariabella. The way she sighed and stretched exactly like her sister made him smile.

"Good morning, lover," she purred.

"Good morning, Bella." He bent and placed a kiss on her forehead. "I have to run back to my place and grab some fresh clothes, okay?"

"You're leaving?" She groaned and became more alert.

"Not for long. I'll be back by the time you're fully awake. Sleep, baby. Rest up. I plan on wearing you out again today."

A sleepy grin stretched over her face and she cuddled up to her pillow. "Don't be gone long, please?"

"Anything for you." With one more kiss to her forehead, he donned his shirt and shoes and headed out.

He stayed on full alert as he walked the narrow streets and then took the stairs to his apartment. The door was still locked, which didn't mean anything. Most Thracians could pick a lock easily enough.

The television was on. He hadn't been watching it. He'd spent most of the weekend with Ariabella.

No surprise, Maxim stepped out of the tiny kitchen, a bowl of cereal in his hands. "It's about time," he said around his food, his Russian accent muffled by crunching. "You're a long way from home, Judah."

Everything in him wanted to lie to Maxim about why he was in Trastevere. His gut insisted. His Thracian blood told him that he was in the presence of someone he shouldn't trust, fellow Thracian or not. "I'm currently on leave from the American Haven. Thought I'd study here for a while." He spoke in English for the first time in weeks. It felt weird after speaking Italian with Ariabella and Bridget for so long.

"I saw what you were studying last night at the club. D'you fuck her?" Maxim's thick black eyebrows lifted.

"It's none of your—"

"I'd fuck her… and her giant sister. Do you know who you were sticking your dick in last night, boy?" He sat down at the table and plopped the bowl down, making it spill over the side. Maxim didn't care. He wanted intel, not to be a courteous guest.

Judah shrugged. "I didn't exactly worry with last names, if you catch my drift." He downplayed the situation as much as possible.

"Grimaldi. As in Xavier Grimaldi's daughters."

Judah made damn sure his aura only revealed the hint of fear Maxim expected at hearing the name. "Can't be. Xavier's daughters all live in the protection of a Haven. They'd be foolish to be among humans."

"Wrong. The two girls you were escorting last night are his oldest daughters. How very coincidental that you should travel halfway around the world and bump into them." His dark eyes studied Judah, making him want to flee.

"You call it coincidental. I call it luck. Why are *you* here, Maxim?" He casually made his way around the room towards the cabinet that held his guns, pretending gather supplies to heat coffee.

"Not that it's any of your concern, but I'm here to check on Xavier's daughters. He was quite worried about them after their brother joined up with the Castilles and has been brainwashed. The boy communicates with the sisters often."

"Does he now?" Judah lit the burner on his small gas stove, placing a pot of hot water on top, careful to keep his voice flat and uninterested in that bit of information.

"We have people who track their correspondences. That's confidential information. Not a word to the sisters."

Judah nodded. "Understood. And you tracked me down, how? Why? I'm on holiday." No one knew he was in Rome except for the man who sent him there. That man wouldn't be so inclined to let anyone know of this mission, especially Maxim the Magician, a man rumored to enjoy hurting women.

"Since you're already here and infiltrated into their lives, I'm sure you will contact me if something happens that I need to know about? Their father would be greatly appreciative."

Maxim brushed right over his question. *Damn it.* "Of course. Should I be looking for anything in particular?"

"Ariabella is in a dangerous line of work. She periodically aids police investigations in a major human trafficking case. The man running the ring is Olympian. He's put out a hit on her, from what I hear." Milk dripped off his chin and he swiped at it with the back of his hand.

Judah's heart hammered in his chest at the thought. He hadn't known *that* piece of information. His initial investigation of Ariabella had uncovered her activities with the humans. It was not something Judah wanted her involved with, even though her gifts had brought down some of the main players, and according to his inside sources, she was the key to bring down Julio Val D'Esta for good. Judah had been trying to figure out who this guy was as hard as the police.

"I didn't know. Like I said, I'm on leave and she happens to be a nice piece of ass. Guess I should pay attention to more than that, huh?" He grinned as he shrugged it off.

The crass words were not lost on Maxim, who viewed women as toys to play with and mutilate. He was that child who killed small animals and cut the heads off dolls and lit cats on fire.

"Guess you should start fucking human women instead. They're much more disposable."

Judah cringed. "Not my thing. I might have to start asking their last names, though." It made him sick to make light of his relationship with Ariabella. It was necessary for her safety. No matter what human scum might be after her, the man sitting at his table was worse by far. And Maxim liked any form of leverage he could acquire.

"Maybe. Then again, I doubt Xavier gives a shit who his daughters screw as long as they breed. If you get to do the other sister, let me know how she is in the sack. She's got a defiant streak." Maxim's snicker gave him a sick feeling in his stomach. "I have to join Prince Avondale in the American Haven. Princess Salina supposedly killed the Grand Deity and Ashton wants me there." He stated the accusation as if it weren't a monumental act, as if it wasn't something that could change the face of their world forever.

Judah would never understand the lack of conscience in Maxim.

"I'm leaving Xavier's daughters in your care, Judah. You might not be in the European chain of command." He shrugged like it didn't matter. "Eh, conveniently, you're here. You will keep the girls in hand and contact me if there is a problem, yes?" He toyed with his spoon and gave him a direct stare.

Judah casually nodded, attempting to match Maxim's level of calm. "Sure. If Xavier wants eyes on all his family, do you have someone assigned to the other sister? She doesn't live here, but she's visiting and I haven't seen anyone."

"He's doing a good job, wouldn't you say?" Maxim chuckled. "Then again, you didn't see me either. Maybe you're losing your touch?" Maxim narrowed his eyes, assessing Judah to the point of making him uncomfortable.

"Men like us need to relax sometime, you know?"

"Men like us don't relax. Ever. Keep your eyes open, Judah.

I would hate for something to happen to a good soldier like you and you're playing with fire."

"Perhaps." Judah nodded his head and bit the interior of his cheek. Something was off, though he couldn't put his finger on it. He tried to recall the people he'd seen since Bridget had been in town. None of them stuck out. None of them had set off his internal alarms. He hadn't detected many other auras and those he had were of people he knew.

Judah was a spy being spied on and that bothered him. It made him question whether this was a legitimate protection detail or something more.

"I'll be in touch." Maxim stood and wiped his bearded mouth. He grabbed a duffle and shoved right past Judah on his way out the door.

Air whooshed out of Judah's lungs when Maxim was gone. What the hell was that about? He showered and gathered his clothes and schoolbooks, aware that he had to keep the façade now more than ever. Every move he made around his apartment was purposely lazy as he covertly searched every inch of his home for hidden cameras and anything out of place. He would have to do the same at Ariabella's.

When he arrived back at her place, the girls sat on the couch with their coffee, talking and laughing. He loved the high, soft sound of Ariabella's happiness. Her voice fit her well; gentle, airy, and full of sunshine. Judah rubbed his chest, the guilt and worry a heavy stone in his heart.

"Are you okay?" Bridget tilted her head to the side and narrowed her eyes.

Judah righted himself and cleared the lump out of his throat, remembering to answer in Italian. "Yeah, totally cool. What are you laughing about?"

Ariabella gave him a side grin. "Bridget was being silly."

"I was not," she protested. "I would love to go visit my precious baby brother…and all his hunky Thracian friends." Bridget wiggled her brows, causing the girls to chuckle again. "Did you see much action at the Thracian center, Judah?" Bridget took a sip of her drink.

"It was fairly unexciting, I'm afraid. My time at the training center was uneventful, nothing like it must be now. I worked out, I studied history, Olympian law, human law, and once they figured out my specialty, I took classes in that area."

Both the girls seemed disappointed with his answer. Fortunately, or unfortunately, depending on your point of view, his years in the Tennessee Haven flew by without any drama or fanfare. Ryse and the other Elites taught him to fight, how to defend their people against exposure and Rogues.

"What would you have done, Judah, if you saw Hermes summoning the Deities?"

"Shit myself, I'm sure." They all got a laugh out of that one. He leaned back in his chair. "I really can't say. I would've loved to be there, to see a god right in front of me. I can't even begin to imagine how cool that would be."

"Our brother was there; he saw Hermes take the Deities up." Ariabella's eyes sparkled when she mentioned Dante and lifted his most recent letter for them to see. "Even now, he's guarding an Oracle sent from Delphi to council the widow of the Grand Deity." She shook her head in amazement. "He's been through so much; finally finding his place with Lady Avery, only to have her killed. Yet he remains strong in his convictions and his Thracian duties. I'm so proud of him. I want you to meet him, Judah. You would get along famously."

"Was this the same brother who sent you the letter the day

we met? The one in love?" Judah reached over and tucked her hair behind her ear as she nodded and a huge smile crossed her face.

Bridget sighed. "Listen, I'm happy for you and Dante both, but come on, share the secret. What's the key to finding a mate? I want to settle down, have babies, teach them English and Italian, and how to use their Olympian gifts. Is that too much to ask for? Am I praying to the wrong god? Maybe Zeus quit making matches. Maybe I need to pray to Hera or Aphrodite?"

Judah let his heart lighten as the two women kept talking about life and the things they wanted out of it.

Funny, his future had been so certain a few weeks ago. Thracian spies didn't have mates or families, they didn't settle down or live like normal people. Up until this mission, he had been resigned to that life of dark loneliness. Now he didn't know if he could give up the woman before him with golden hair and sunshine in her smile. He didn't want to be alone anymore, not when he knew Ariabella existed.

Fatherhood hadn't been on his mind—*ever*—but now it was, because he had a woman who would want kids. Judah had no idea what it took to be a father. His parents had abandoned him at birth, his mother gladly handing over her newborn to be raised as a Thracian by a foster family. The gift from Ares had skipped his father, making the man angry at the gods for depriving him of what he considered his right. Judah often thought that Ares knew even before his father's birth that he didn't deserve to be a Thracian, which meant that even before Judah was born, Ares saw favor in him.

"The gods know what they're doing," Judah said to Bridget. "They see more than we could ever comprehend. Our vision is restricted and colored by the nonsense of this world. The gods don't have that distraction. Don't worry, beautiful, your mate is out there. You'll know him when you find him."

"Are you sure you don't have a brother?" Bridget sighed. "I'd even take a trusted friend, as long as he's somewhat like you."

Judah threw his head back and laughed. "I'll be thinking about someone for you."

Bridget held out her hand to seal the pact. "Deal."

"You're an Air Elemental, right?" He filtered through other Elementalists he knew.

She nodded, wiggled her fingers at him, and an unnatural wind ruffled his hair.

"I'll keep that in mind." He had a growing affection for Bridget, and when she left that afternoon, he hugged her close and told her to be safe and take Dante's advice, trust no one. Maybe the boy was in over his head with the Castilles and had done something to make his family a target? Dante knew something they didn't. Either way, it was sound advice.

Judah might not know exactly what was going on in the undercurrent of the Olympian world, but he could try his best to protect Ariabella and Bridget...especially from Maxim.

CHAPTER FIVE

BRIDGET WAS BACK IN TRASTEVERE ONLY A FEW DAYS LATER. UNLIKE before, this visit was not about fun and dancing.

Today, the gods had beckoned.

Today, history would be made.

Today was judgment day.

Judah, Ariabella, and Bridget stood in a crowded line of Olympians. Not knowing who was tailing Bridget, he scanned the crowd of people over and over again. Men, women, children, Olympians of all ages congregated around the entrance of the Colosseum.

That morning, Maxim had called to check in on him. "Keep

the girl close," he'd said. "You never know how people will react to the execution. Xavier might need her to be brought in."

"I will. The other sister is here also. I will keep her close."

"My man will take care of her. Get her to the Colosseum." Maxim hung up without any closing words.

Judah did as he was told, along with many of their fellow Olympians.

Humans would walk under the arches and into a ruin of rocks and see vegetation covered paths from history and stories of old. They would never see the marvels that Olympians could see. The Colosseum was a portal to one of the European Havens. As Judah crossed the threshold, he nodded at the Thracian security guard working the tour lines. The second he penetrated the barrier of Olympic energy protecting the arena, the world changed. No longer was the Colosseum a piece of rubble from history, but a wonderfully protected, complete structure, bustling with Olympians who hurried to find a seat.

Human eyes would never comprehend the science or magic behind the Havens. It often boggled his mind that two worlds could inhabit the same space. Where he stood, there might be a human in the same spot taking pictures or marveling at the structure. As soon as an Olympian entered the Haven, they were gone from human eyes and minds.

The Havens were safe places for their people, covered by the power of the gods, and protected by magic so deep and potent, it seeped into the soil like rain water. It made Judah proud of his heritage, proud of the blood that ran through his veins.

"We're late. My family will be seated by now." Ariabella texted her mother to find out their location. They walked through the stone halls and waited for a response. "They'll be close to the bottom."

It was the first information about her other family members she'd mentioned. Acting like he didn't know anything about her, Judah turned her chin to him so she had to look into his eyes. "Why would your family be sitting close to the bottom?"

Olympians had a social structure much like the ancients did. Ariabella and Bridget's father was the commander of armies and the protector of Prince Ashton Avondale, the Deity Prince of their country. General Xavier's family would be prominently seated close to the arena floor, among those of nobility and purest blood.

Ariabella swallowed hard and glanced over at Bridget, who nodded her consent. "Our family name," she tiptoed up and whispered in his ear, "is Grimaldi."

Though Judah knew this secret from the moment he took this job, the confirmation of it still hit him hard. He closed his eyes and made sure to react as expected. He grit his teeth, "As in *Xavier* Grimaldi? You're the daughters of a fucking General?" Judah's glare darted between the girls. He stepped close to them and lowered his voice. At least now he could express his dislike for this situation. "And you picked *now* to tell me? When we're in a horde of people and I can't adequately protect you?"

"It's not a big deal, Judah. No one knows us. Don't be angry, please?" Her bright brown eyes begged for his forgiveness.

"I'm a Thracian, you comprehend that, right?" Both girls nodded. "I may be from America, yet your father still outranks me. If anything happens to you—"

"Nothing is going to happen," Bridget said, grabbing him none too gently on the arm.

A blast of power pulsed through the arena like an atomic blast. The pull of the aura was enough to rob him of breath. People in the halls all rushed into the seats to see where the power came from. Judah was one of them. He grabbed the girls' arms and dragged them into the arena. "It's begun. We don't have time to find your family."

They scrambled to get any seat they could, regardless of the view.

"What's happened?" Bridget's mouth hung open as she stared at the arena floor with wide eyes.

Men and women—noblemen, if he had to guess—stood above a bloody lamb as it took its last breath and collapsed. Judah knew the rituals and recognized the blooded lamb as a sacrifice to the gods. "They have to offer up a sacrifice for the gods to come to this world. Look." Judah pointed at the giant woman who stepped out of the portal.

The entire arena fell as still as the grave. No one drew breath.

She stood at least three feet taller than the noblemen who had called her forth. Her dark chocolate-colored hair flowed in wild curls down her front and back. A spread of peacock feathers adorned her golden crown. That same gold covered a tall staff decorated with jewels and carved to mimic the rounded peacock feather. Necklaces of glittering jewels hung from her neck down her chest, over her bare shoulders, and every which way. They connected to bracelets on one arm and were linked to a ring on her opposite hand. Jewels reflected the light and sparkled with every move she made. The rich purple of her gown was fitting for the one they called the Queen of the Gods.

"Hera," Ariabella whispered in awe, clutching Judah's arm. Her huge, wide eyes met his.

The name started to spread like wildfire. Everyone who caught it sent it on until the stadium was chanting *Hera, Hera, Hera.*

The goddess cast her gaze over all the crowd then took a low, graceful bow.

Cheers erupted and applause filled the air. As Hera righted herself, her wide lips curved into a smile so radiant, it could shadow the sun. Judah was so enamored with her that he almost neglected to see the six hulking Thracians who accompanied her.

The noblemen scurried out of their way as they set a perimeter around the goddess.

Hera waved her staff at the portal and it stretched, filling the entire basin of the arena like a pool of water. It bubbled and boiled until out of its depths came a scene.

"What is that?" Bridget squinted down at the floor of the arena.

"It's the Haven in North America," said a man on the row in front of them. "That's where the execution is taking place. See." He pointed out the people as he named them. "There's the Grand Deity's widow Dynasty, the Prince Hayden, and there are our Deities, Charles and Filene Avondale with Prince Ashton."

"Master Ryse Castille." Judah found the name uttered from his lips before the thought finished in his mind. The sight of his Master Thracian still sent chills down his spine. Ryse was a force of nature, amplified by the gifts of the gods and armed with a blade forged by the hands of Ares himself. Beholding him in this manner, as a true executioner, made Judah want to fall to his knees in servitude.

"Judah?" Ariabella cupped his cheek. "You're pale. Are you all right?"

Her touch brought him out of his trance and he nodded, unable to speak. Drawing her under his arm, he moved between the girls, knowing they would both need support before this was all over. Ariabella wrapped her arms around his waist and Bridget accepted his outstretched hand.

Someone was about to die. No one needed to face that alone.

"Behold," Hera said, her arms outstretched to the unfolding scene. "Your gods have come to walk among you, that you will witness our justice and our mercies. We have not forgotten our people and we see the desires of your hearts. Today, we honor those who shall reign and rebuke those who have turned away. Watch, Olympians of Roma, and know who holds your destiny." She pointed her staff at the waters in the pool and they disappeared, leaving behind a vision of the Tennessee Haven so real, Judah wondered if he could touch the people on stage.

Zeus, a god of gold and majesty, presided over the execution.

"There's Father." Bridget pulled on his arm, knowing better than to speak too loudly. If people around identified them as Xavier's daughters, and things went badly, they could be harmed by the mob. Bridget's frightened eyes met his and he gripped her hand tighter.

"Dante. It's him. I see him. He's cut his hair." Ariabella covered her opened mouth.

Judah followed her gaze to the man. He had a general knowledge of Dante's looks, and now he could examine him. The man was a beast, well over six and a half feet tall. His eyes were what stood out. They were the same sand color as his hair. No wonder he'd lived in a Haven his entire life. A giant with unique eyes would stand out anywhere in the world.

"See how he sits among the Elites," Ariabella whispered. "Holiest Zeus, I'm so proud of him." She blinked back tears as Judah pressed a kiss to her forehead.

"I'm guessing we missed the fanfare of introductions." It

didn't matter; Judah and everyone in that arena knew the players of the game.

Sitting on a pyramid of platforms was the Lady Dynasty. Beneath her, on a lower stair, sat her son Hayden and a lovely lady in white with black hair. If his research was accurate, this was Dante's Belle, the Oracle Lysandra. There were two empty chairs on the opposite side of Hayden and the Oracle that he assumed would be filled by Ryse and someone else.

Sitting on the stage level, as if guarding them all, were the Elites. From left to right sat Cutter, an ancient swordsman of old, Philippe, an Italian Elementalist who was madly popular in this part of the world—especially with the ladies—then sat former Deity Hammon of Africa, whose tracking powers and abilities were noted throughout their history. On the other side of the aisle sat Samuel, a general badass jackass who people either loved or hated. Mainly hated. Next was Brenden, the shapeshifting beast whose blood made him a mutt in more ways than one. And on the end, closest to the gods, was Dante.

Judah could understand how Ariabella and Bridget could be so proud. To have a place on that stage, with those men, meant that you had achieved the greatest honor a Thracian could wish for: to be *Elite*.

"Father hates them, those warriors." Bridget pointed out the men who he'd been thinking about. "He says they have no honor, that they are murderers for murder's sake."

"I don't believe that," Ariabella spit out with passion. "Do you honestly think that Dante would associate with them if they were like that? He's written us letters, told us all about them. They are virtuous people, Bridget. We don't know the whole story, and neither does Father."

"It's not right." Bridget shook her head. "Father is over there as if he opposes his own Master."

The arena went silent as Zeus held up his hands to speak.

"Before we carry out this sentencing, we would like to right a wrong committed against the house of Castille. During her capture, Salina Avondale took the life of the newly bonded Divine Grace, Avery McClain. Avery's soul has rested in the hands of the gods. However, we know that a Deity will need his Grace to rule by his side. In a measure to show our faith in the Thracian soldiers and the Olympian race, the gods deliver Avery back into the world of the living."

Those in the arena gasped and covered their eyes as bright white lightning shot into the sky. A torrent of red clouds swirled around and around, funneling down to the stage.

"Oh my god," Ariabella said. "They're bringing her back to life."

"Have the gods ever done such a thing?" Judah's skeptical mind was turning at the implications of this move. The gods were undoing death, and Hades didn't like to be cheated out of a turn.

"Not that I can recall. Dante is so happy; see his face?"

Sure enough, her brother grinned and joined the rest of the Thracians who stood and applauded the actions of Zeus. They all seemed happy. What had this girl done in such a short time to garner the affections of the Elites? *She must be special.*

The Divine Grace arose from a whirlwind of flames, her body like a struck match. She was magnificent, even Judah had to admit it. Avery wasn't his type, even though her dark blood-red curls and unearthly good looks had the jaw of every man and woman in the Colosseum hanging open.

"You have to give her credit." Bridget grinned and applauded as the Deity couple of Avery and Ryse raised their hands in the air. "The girl knows how to make an entrance."

Judah and Ariabella grinned and clapped along with the crowd. Ariabella's joy was for her brother. Surprisingly, Judah felt the same joy. It made him stop for a moment.

Most of the Thracians who served under General Xavier eventually heard his theory about how Ryse, who should have been an only son, had a brother. There were many different rumors floating about. Some said Dynasty had an affair with a Thracian, which accounted for Ryse being both Deity and Thracian. Some said that Hayden was the product of infidelity. Judah could only make up his own mind based on what he knew: Dynasty was loyal to the gods and her husband. Ryse and his brother, Hayden, were clones of their father and held too much of a resemblance to Dynasty to not be her children.

Conclusion: the Castilles were unique in many ways.

He turned his gaze to the opposite side of the stage where the European Deities sat, also watching Avery with amazement. While the father and mother were supposedly friends of the Castilles, the son and daughter were not fans. Ashton and Salina Avondale had done little to hide their disdain for the family so favored by the gods. The hatred Judah saw on General Xavier's face was also right there for the world to see. If the gods had blessed the Castilles, not the Avondales, and Maxim worked directly for Ashton, did that mean his motives might be in question? Was his mission for the betterment and protection of Ariabella, or for something else entirely? Did his orders come from Maxim or a higher station? Who was behind it? And if General Xavier was so worried about his daughters' lives, why didn't he contact them directly and force them to go back to the safety of a Haven?

Instead, it was Dante who reached out to tell Ariabella to be careful and Maxim who secretly put trackers on them.

"Bridget," he said, watching General Xavier's face as Avery bowed to her husband. "Has your father been in contact with you about any of this?"

"Not really. Why?" Her attention was on the stage, not his question. She had her arms folded in front of her, her eyes narrowed at something below.

"I'm wondering why not. It's kind of a big deal."

Bridget waved him off. "Eh, Father is always up Ashton's ass. He hasn't made time for us in years. We're lucky to get a card on our birthdays."

Yet the General was worried enough to have the girls guarded? It didn't add up.

"Your mind is working on something." Ariabella touched his cheek, turning his head away from the execution and making him lock eyes with her. "What's wrong?"

"I don't know yet." Judah pressed a kiss to her forehead.

The entire time they watched the trial and execution, he tried desperately to put pieces of the puzzle together. Were the girls in danger from their own father? If Maxim had someone tailing Bridget, and possibly Ariabella, there was no way in hell it was done out of concern for their well-being. Maxim didn't understand that concept. Judah's orders came from the American General. Falcon hadn't explained much and he didn't have to. *Watch the girl. Keep her safe. I'll check in as necessary.* Falcon sent the information over and that was the extent of his orders. Who had given Falcon the order? Ryse was the only person higher on the chain of command. Was it him? *Dear Zeus.* The air left his lungs in a rush at the thought of being on a mission directly from the Master Thracian. Couldn't be. Ryse wouldn't care about Xavier's daughters. He had much bigger issues at the moment. Had their brother pulled some strings? Asked a favor from the General? Who in the hell had truly given him the orders?

"*Santo cielo*, he really did it." Ariabella buried her face in Judah's shirt after the grand blade sliced through Salina's neck.

Judah couldn't take his eyes off the gruesome scene before him. Princes Salina Avondale was dead by the hand of the Master Thracian. Truly, history had been made that day. Judah cringed as the Divine Grace, Filene, wailed for her daughter. The parents of the princess were overcome with grief. What parent wouldn't be?

The people in the arena, all of whom were under the care of the European Deities, booed and hissed. They even threw things into the image as if they could hit Master Ryse. Judah's instincts said to get the girls out of the crowd before riots broke out. Too bad he couldn't move.

"She was our Princess." Bridget wiped her eyes. "They—"

Her words were cut short by the storm that gathered over the stage. Judah instinctively pulled the women closer to his side as a vile aura filled the Colosseum. He surveyed the people around, looking for one who might be causing the upset and the person tracking Bridget. Whoever it was, they wouldn't want to lose her in this crowd.

As oily winds wrapped around them, transcending time and space to cross into their Haven, the people crouched down, covering themselves from the evil that whirled and swirled about them.

Hades.

"This one belongs to me."

The smoky figure of the ruler of the underworld formed horizontally above Salina and breathed her in, inhaling her body like a fume and taking her essence into his.

Judah swallowed hard, observing as Hades spoke to Master Ryse, wondering how in the name of the gods any man had the courage to stare down the father of demons and hell-fire. That was what made Ryse the Master of all Thracians. He was powerful enough to take on the gods and win. Did the gods realize they had created a being in him that could ultimately be their rival?

Hades vanished, taking the Princess and every drop of Salina's blood with him.

"I've never seen a god in all my life," Bridget mused beside him. "Today, I've seen my fair share, and I can honestly say I never want to see Hades again."

"I second that." Judah released the girls from his hold and again glanced around the crowd to see if anyone was paying them attention. A woman two rows back met his eyes then skirted away. She held the arm of a man; both appeared focused on the scene before them. It could be coincidence. They both had black hair and dark eyes, like many Italians. They could very well be natives. Still, he kept them in the back of his mind. There was no telling who Maxim put as a tail on Bridget. It could've been a woman and Maxim purposely tried to throw Judah off by referring to her as a him.

Judah put nothing past Maxim…and now, watching General Xavier, he couldn't help question his assignment by Maxim. Xavier glared at Ryse with true malice in his eyes. His nostrils flared and his lips pressed into a thin line.

"Your father looks very angry over Salina's death," Judah whispered to Ariabella. "Were they close?"

"It's possible. He's always been Ashton's guardian, so he practically helped raise them both."

"Is your father a man to keep secrets?"

Her big brown eyes met his. "He's the guardian of a

rebellious prince." A deep groove formed between her brows and she skirted her gaze away. "I'm sure he has many secrets."

"What aren't you telling me, Bella?"

Ariabella's eyes pinpointed her father and she shook her head. Her lips trembled as she spoke. "I don't know if my father is a guiltless man, Judah. I see my brother down there, sitting alongside the Elites, devoted to a Divine Grace who was given life by the gods, and in high favor of the Master Thracian. His life is blessed, no doubt. You can see the fruits. Then there is my father, literally on the opposing side." A tear ran down her cheek.

Ariabella's sadness broke his heart. He loved this woman and would do anything to protect her from the cold, hard truth.

She stared longingly at her father. "I have to wonder if he has not chosen the wrong path."

Judah checked his phone to make sure he didn't have orders. This crowd was not happy about the events and it wouldn't surprise him if the daughter of the General needed to go into hiding. He prayed that no one recognized them.

"There's Mother. I found her." Bridget pointed to the opposite side of the arena where the nobility sat in a prime location, right by the base.

Their mother was surrounded by her other eight daughters, who were a blend of Bridget's tall, willowy features and Ariabella's petite, dainty characteristics. They all had the same basic facial structure and couldn't deny their relatives. All the girls were in their first century of life, young by Olympian standards.

Their mother, an older, heavier-set version of Bridget, wiped tears from her eyes and covered her mouth with her hand. She said something to one of the girls, who shook her head, vigorously denying whatever the mother had spoken. It didn't help the despair on the woman's face.

As Zeus, Ares, Athena, and Poseidon named Hayden Castille the Grand Deity, to be crowned in a month's time, the people of nobility sitting in the boxes had mixed reactions. Judah couldn't contain his shock as Charles Avondale supported the much younger, less experienced prince. What had transpired in Heaven when the Deities were called up?

Some people booed, some clapped and nodded, some hurled food and trash at the images of the gods. This country followed the Avondales, and while they might be devoted to the gods, they were also proud of the modern perfection their Deities portrayed. Their beloved Deity had passed the ultimate crown of power to a *Castille*.

The day was full of revelations.

At last, Hera sent the images away in a wave of water and stood before the crowd. Her jewel-colored gown and adornments sparkled in the golden rays of late afternoon sunlight, making her seem all the more surreal.

"Olympians of Europe, those of you in the Colosseum and those who have seen these events from your homes, I see into your hearts."

Everything stilled. It was like the whole world had gotten caught with their hand in the cookie jar. Hera's shining face held a mixture of anger and understanding, as if she pitied the foolish people around the arena. She knew details of the situation these Olympians could never comprehend. She had the knowledge of the ages, the understanding of the universe only a god could comprehend—a burden only a god could bear.

"You treasure your Deities, as you should. However, do not let the people in leadership be your only compass. It is up to each individual to seek the will of the gods no matter your circumstances. Be in constant prayer of the decisions you make and you shall hear the voices of the gods guiding you." She placed a hand over her heart and her face softened. "You are our chosen. You, Olympians of the world, are our children and we care for you. Let today serve as a reminder to those who doubt our existence. We see you. We hear you. And we shall chasten you as any parent would, out of love. The other gods ascend back to the Heavens, whereas I, Hera, goddess of the gods and mother to all, wish to tarry a while and be with my children. Please, send me your young, that I may dote on the most blessed of our race." She opened her arms and a sweet, warm wind glided over the people, filled with the kindness of her aura.

Children flocked to the pit of the arena, running as fast as they could to embrace the goddess. She knelt on the grass in order to hug them, kiss them, speak blessings over them, then sent them to their parents glowing with the light she shed.

There were over eighty thousand people filling the Colosseum to its max capacity, yet Hera stayed until the sun had left the sky, the lights came on, and every child had received a blessing. The love she held for her people radiated on her face.

Thousands took their leave once their children were seen, only needing that taste of her presence to be filled. Some left immediately, as if to escape the goddess's attention. He didn't blame them. Judah found himself torn between getting Ariabella out of the crowds and receiving his own direction from Hera. Luckily, Bridget and Ariabella were in no hurry to leave either. They stayed until only a few hundred people were left.

Hera's heavenly guardians kept an eye on every person who approached the goddess. They didn't seem overly friendly. In fact, they were more like statues than actual security. Their auras were potent, creating a visible layer of protection.

"When a Thracian dies on this earth," Judah said, thinking

out loud, "there is no greater honor than to serve as a guardian to the gods. Those men must have been mighty warriors in life to be the protectors of Hera." He smiled down at Ariabella, not needing to say how badly he hoped he was honored in death. She understood, touching his cheek with a comforting hand.

"I would like to get closer," Bridget said.

Judah cringed internally as they made their way closer to the pit floor, deeper into the crowds, where they might be recognized. Judah pulled the hood of his sweatshirt over his head and made Ariabella and Bridget cover up with scarves and a hat he'd brought. He could blend in, be practically unnoticeable to people sitting right next to him. It was his gift. The girls were high-born Olympians with strong auras and recognizable facial features.

"Why are you acting so strange?" Bridget said, turning her nose up at him.

"I don't like crowds, not even Olympian crowds." Judah kept his head down while keeping his senses open to everything around him. Auras mixed and mingled, emotions trickling out like water leaks. The people had let their guard down with a goddess nearby. That didn't mean danger couldn't find them.

Hera now walked through the throng, touching people, praying over others. She mingled about the people with no fear, no worry in the world, and only a kind smile on her face.

"I almost overlooked you, Judah." Her angelic voice caressed his ears. He swallowed hard and stared way up to meet her eyes. "Not a surprise."

"My goddess." He nodded his head. How did she know his name? Out of the entire crowd, she spoke *his* name. Shivers ran up his spine.

"The workings of the gods favor you." She bent low at her waist to speak directly to him and Ariabella. "Sweet children, remember, truth is still truth, though your perception is skewed. The lies you know shall turn to bitter truth. The truth you know shall seem to be lies if not viewed through the eyes of love. Everything you share shall be challenged and torn apart if you lean on your own understandings of what is true or what is false. Trust the gods have been at work here and you shall not go astray if you keep faith." To Bridget, she said, "You, child, must never cease to fight for the desires of your heart." Hera smiled and cupped the side of Bridget's face. "You have much to offer."

With nothing more than the nod of her head, Hera passed them by, on to the next worshipers.

"Can we go now?" Judah wrestled with his impatience and what Hera's message might mean. He was overwhelmed by the aura of the goddess and the uncomfortable crowds. He feared that everything Hera said was right. If that was the case, Ariabella was going to find out in the next few days all the lies he had been hiding.

⟵⸱ ⸱⸱ ⸱⟶

Ariabella hugged Bridget goodbye late that night. "I'm sorry to see you go. I feel like we need to be together after today."

"Me too. Unfortunately, I have to work in the morning and I still have a three-hour drive home. I'll call you tomorrow when we've both had a chance to digest all this." Bridget also hugged Judah before she left. "Thanks for taking care of us today." She winked and headed out the door, her tear tracks still visible on her face.

Ariabella waited a few seconds before she went into Judah's arms. He kissed her hard, plunging his tongue into her mouth and winding his hands into her hair. "I want you," he murmured against her lips, lifting her blouse over her head. "Now."

The feeling was mutual. After an emotionally draining day, she wanted to feel his strength, feel his body moving inside her. Her fingers made quick work of his shirt buttons and she bit her bottom lip when Judah dipped to lavish his attentions on her breasts. She loved his lips, especially when they met her skin and set it on fire.

Judah liked her to be on top and she, too, favored that position. He was such a large man compared to her, and when he covered her body, she thought he could crush her. When she rode him, she felt powerful, as if on the back of a wild stallion running free. They didn't bother going to the bedroom; Ariabella took him right on the couch.

"My Bella," he said in her ear, holding her hips as she ground down on him. "I'll do anything to make you happy."

Ariabella pressed a kiss to his sweaty brow. "Silly man, I'm already happy. Don't worry. You? You make me excited, joyous, and a million other sublime things." She grinned and let her head fall backwards, her long hair tickling the upper curves of her bottom.

Judah picked up the pace until they both were panting, taken deep within the throes of passion. He was perfect inside her. When she was in his arms, she felt like her small body had been made to fit his like a glove. Judah's strong arms lifted her easily, helping her move up and down when her knees shook and her thighs trembled under the pressure building from her core. She whispered his name; begging or praising, she didn't know. All the lines blurred with Judah. Feeling his body coil tight and then spring free inside her was by far the most glorious experience she ever had. Making love to Judah turned her brain to mush and all she could concentrate on was doing whatever it took to drive him mad.

Once she succeeded, Ariabella lay on his chest, running her

fingers over his warm skin, allowing their hearts to stop racing. "Why were you so edgy today?"

Her body moved up and down with his heavy breath. "I don't like crowds and that was a high-emotion situation. People are unpredictable, Bella. You can't trust a mob. Oh, and let's not forget that you're the daughter of a bloody general."

Ariabella raised her head to look at him. "Would you have talked to me, had you known?"

"In a heartbeat." The grin that graced his face made her insides tingle. "I am a man, after all, and you're the sexiest damn thing I've ever seen."

Ariabella laughed and rolled her eyes. She lay back down and they were silent for a while until she spoke into the darkness. "I've never seen anyone beheaded before, have you?"

Judah cleared his throat. "Not like that."

Ariabella rested her chin on the back of her hand. "How, then?"

"In fights, battles, nothing as…planned as a true execution."

"Have you fought many battles, Judah?"

He propped his head up with an arm. "I've mainly been in hand-to-hand situations. Being born Thracian equates to a life of combat and training for combat. It's part of who I am, who the gods created me to be."

She swallowed, wondering if she should even ask her next question. "Ha—Have you killed people?"

His brown eyes met hers. "Do you want the weight of my answer on your shoulders?"

"That's a yes." Ariabella's blood ran cold.

He averted his gaze. "Be careful what you ask me, Bella. You can drill me for truth, but you might not want to know it."

Ariabella laid her cheek against his chest once more,

knowing there were secrets within Judah that only time could reveal. She wouldn't force him, couldn't force him. If they were to be mated, they had to have true trust, the kind her powers didn't betray.

"What do you think Hera's message meant?"

"I, um, I'm not sure." His fingers trailed up and down her back. "Your gifts are all about finding the truth. In some ways, mine is too."

"What if it means my gifts will be wrong? That they fail me? I've always depended on my powers, then Dante warned me against it, now Hera." She met his eyes once more. "It makes me question my judgment."

"I'll try not to take that personally." Judah grinned, melting her heart.

"Not about you, Judah. You're the best thing that has ever happened to me." Ariabella stretched up to kiss him and felt his heart speed up under her palm.

"You're my sunshine, Bella." Judah tried to cover his yawn. There was no hiding it.

"Come on." She stood and pulled him to his feet. "Your sunshine needs to give way to the moon for a while. Let's get some sleep."

Ariabella curled up in bed with Judah, noting how he quickly relaxed into sleep. She, on the other hand, couldn't get Hera's words out of her head. If her gifts betrayed her, what else could she believe?

It took Ariabella almost an hour before Judah felt the tension slip out of her shoulders. Hera's words had made her anxious and worried. By the time she finally fell asleep, he had a limited window to get the information he needed.

Judah slid out of her arms and quietly went into the living room to check the trackers he'd put on Bridget. The receiver in her car was at her house, along with the one in her wallet and the one in the cardigan she carried everywhere with her.

He pulled up the information on Val D'Esta and his latest movements: nothing. The guy was a ghost. There were no pictures of him on news sites, no records, nothing. It was like he showed up, grabbed a bunch of women, and vanished. The fact that Maxim knew of him only made the situation worse. The guy was pure evil. The other problem was, Judah had a gut instinct that there was more to this case and he couldn't put the pieces together.

Judah dug through her purse, sifted through her desk, even tried to find something on her laptop; anything that would help him discover what Val D'Esta looked like, where he might be, *anything*.

He came up short.

Where did she keep her files? This was gaining him nothing but a guilty conscience.

From the doorway of her room, he watched her sleep. Even in the dark, she glowed with an inner light he couldn't explain.

He loved her.

That was the only thing that could explain the aching in his heart when he looked at her, or the completeness he felt when they made love.

He loved her.

"What's wrong?" Her sleepy voice pulled him from his revelation. Ariabella sat up and pushed her mass of golden hair off her face. "Judah?"

"I love you."

Ariabella's eyes widened, the sleep clearing in an instant. She became fully alert at his words. "You what?"

Judah sat down on the edge of her bed and rested his elbows on his knees, his back to her as he said it again, "I love you, Bella."

"Why do you say that like you're confessing a crime?" She looped her arms around his neck from behind, rubbing his chest. "Talk to me."

As much as he wanted to truly confess his crimes, Maxim's appearance raised the stakes. The clear divide between Ariabella's father and the gods had raised the stakes. He gave her a truth that would do until she needed to know the rest.

"My entire life, my actions have been dictated to me by my superior officers. I've followed orders as long as I was old enough to understand them. Yet, when I think about someone ordering me away from you, it makes me worry that I won't have the strength to follow through."

"Did someone call? Do you have orders?" Ariabella's voice pitched higher than normal. Her breathing sped up.

"Nothing happened. Not yet. There's always another mission, though. Always a chance that they could call me in and ship me off to some hell hole." The very thought of losing her made his chest tighten in pain. The threat was real, as real as whatever he was protecting her from at the moment. He didn't have the strength to leave her behind.

Ariabella moved to the floor in front of him, cradling his head between her hands. "How do we stop it? How do we keep them for taking you away? Or," her shoulders bunched up, "do I prepare to go with you? I'll do anything, Judah, anything to be with you."

He shook his head, hating the idea that she would give up

her life to follow him…and humbled by it at the same time. "Thracians are at the mercy of their generals, especially men like me. I have no family, nothing to tie me to any one place. They ship me around the world because I'm a free man. My parents are dead. I have no home to speak of. I'm a drifter."

"I'll be your home. I'll be your family. Me and Bridget." The innocent love on her face only enslaved his heart even more. "Wherever you go, I go. Or…I'll wait for you…wherever we want to live."

"Your family?"

"Will be happy to see me when we visit." A glorious smile stretched over her face.

"I'll never be able to thank the gods enough for you." He ran his knuckles down her cheek, loving the silk of her skin.

"Whatever brought you to Trastevere was no accident, Judah. I've been waiting for you my whole life."

He rested his forehead against hers. Gods, if she only knew the truth of what brought him here…or who.

CHAPTER SIX

After the execution, the Olympian world was on high alert, especially Judah. He did his best to act normal for Ariabella, however, his senses were acute to the details of their life. Along with checking out every person that crossed their path, he monitored Bridget closely.

Judah tapped in to some of his sources around the world to keep up with the comings and goings of all the Deities, who was moving against whom, and any new activity from the Rogues. The day after the execution, a huge Olympian clinic in Chicago was raided, resulting in the deaths of dozens of innocent people. The compound was owned by Evander Castille, a cousin of the Deities.

He died in the raid, a true loss for Olympians who came to him for aid.

Another location, a seemingly random Olympian community in South America, was attacked and set on fire. While the death toll was low, the number of missing persons was questionably high.

Prince Ashton was rumored to be behind both the raids and that only amped up Judah's nerves. He caught himself being exceptionally quiet when Ariabella talked about the Avondales with high regards. She chalked it up to him being American. The truth was, Judah had met Prince Ashton and Princess Salina many years ago while in Thracian training. Even then, he remembered feeling uneasy about their presence, as if at any moment, they could lash out and hurt someone for no other reason than exhibiting their powers.

For the next several days, Judah covertly gathered intel about Dante, the Elites, and their activities. Something fishy was going on and he had to get to the bottom of it. To add to his stress, Dante called her and Judah listened in. Her brother told the girls to get somewhere safe, somewhere secret that no one knew of, not even their parents. Ariabella promised she would…then Edgar called.

Ariabella had another interrogation, one that was crucial because they might finally have a picture of Val D'Esta. What was worse, he knew the second she lied to Judah about it.

Ariabella slipped on one of her typical sundresses. "I think today, while you're at school, I'm going to meet one of my girlfriends in Bracciano. There's a café down there we like, right on the lake."

Judah allowed her the lie, knowing the necessity of it, and

used it to justify his own sins. "Will you be back tonight? I've be-come accustomed to having dinner with you, lover."

"I should. You know how women are, though. I'm not going to promise anything." She bit her lip and shrugged. Ariabella grabbed a bright-colored tote out of her closet that he'd never noticed before. She left her usual purse behind and Judah cursed himself for not paying closer attention. Granted, there were at least twenty tote bags and purses in her closet. The problem was, he didn't have a tracker in that bag.

She needed to take her purse. Judah picked it up off the hook and handed it to her like it was no big deal. "I guess I'll have to have a drink with the guys, then come wait for you."

"I don't need that one. Thanks, though." She tossed the purse on the kitchen table.

Shit. He had to get that tracker in her other bag.

"Don't be alarmed if you come home to a naked man in your bed."

Ariabella gasped and closed her eyes, her hand going to her chest. The instant desire in her aura blew over him in a wave of hot lust. "Judah. How am I supposed to concentrate on anything with such an image in my mind?"

Pulling her close, he scooped her up and sat her on the table. He nuzzled her neck and nibbled her ear, making her sigh. "I don't want you to think about anything except me."

Ariabella's head fell to the side and he lavished her neck with kisses and bites. While she was distracted, he scraped the small black patch off her wallet and tried to figure out where he could place it on her new bag. It was so brightly colored with pinks and oranges that a black patch would be noticeable, even as tiny as it was.

"Damn it, Judah. I promised her I'd come."

"What if *I* promise that you'll come?" Judah had to think fast. He shoved his hand up her dress and gripped her bottom. He quickly smoothed the patch of fabric over on her panties. As long as she didn't see her backside, she shouldn't find it or feel it.

Because he was a man, and a dog, he slipped his fingers under the lace and into her slick desire. Ariabella gasped against his lips. All it took was his kiss to get her hot and ready. He loved that about her. For a moment, he allowed himself to get lost in her passion. The way she panted and melted around his penetrating fingers, building to an orgasm so fast, he barely had to try. The airy way she moaned his name when she came almost made him forget that they were both deceiving each other.

Judah stood upright and stepped away, licking his fingers and adjusting his jeans. He glanced at his watch and groaned. "I have class." The irritation in his voice was genuine.

His woman sat there flush-faced with her mouth hanging open, her eyes full of dazed desire and her dress hiked up to her waist. "Huh?" She blinked and giggled. "I think I need to change my panties—"

"No!" Judah had to think fast. "Keep them on. I want you thinking about that all day so you'll hurry back for more."

Ariabella bit her bottom lip, considering. "You know how to keep a woman on the hook." She shook her head, slid off the table, and righted her dress. "My taxi is probably waiting. I'll be home as fast as possible. I want you waiting in my bed and naked, so I can return the favor." She winked at him, slapped a quick kiss on his cheek, and zipped out the door before either one of them could further tease the other.

Judah had her on his GPS tracker. He tailed her for an hour, not north to Bracciano, but south, to Frosinone. She must have gotten out of the taxi because her tracker slowed down, and by the time he caught up to her, she was walking down the street. He followed that brightly colored bag until it disappeared into a hotel.

Judah made his taxi pull over and wait. It was easy for him to hack into the hotel's security cameras and he flipped through the feeds until he saw Ariabella at the front desk. She hadn't rented a room; simply picked up a key and headed up stairs. Scrolling through the other feeds, he saw her bag as it disappeared into a room.

"What are you doing, my sneaky little lover?" he mused. Only minutes later, a dark-headed woman with deep brown curly hair and a dress suit came out of the room. She looked quite different than his dainty blond, much heavier and more serious. The padding under her clothes might fool any number of people. Not Judah. Her large sunglasses covered much of her face and the shoulder pads in the dress jacket made her appear bulkier than normal. Even her gait was different in the pointed high heels.

To an uninterested passerby, this disguise could easily work. Judah, however, knew every nuance of his woman.

Judah had his own bag of tricks. He sprayed gray in his beard, applied sticky prosthetics that made him look like he had crow's feet around his eyes and fake teeth that gave him a slight overbite. He donned a brown cardigan and used a collapsible walking stick as a cane. Old man Judah slipped right into the flow of people and followed her into the police station.

A tall, older man with dark skin met her outside. "Ready?" He handed her a briefcase and opened the door.

"*Sempre.*" Always. Ariabella had even lowered the pitch of her voice in order to complete her transformation.

Judah followed her until she went to a restricted area of the station. There was no way for him to go further without a distraction or a damn good reason to be detained. He didn't think this trip was worth it. Instead, he glanced around and asked someone for the closest hotel, like a lost tourist.

For over an hour, Judah waited in the restaurant across the street, watching for Ariabella to come out. Finally, she and her tall friend stepped into the mid-day sun. Judah left cash on the table and grabbed an abandoned newspaper. He sauntered right up behind them, shielding his aura so tight, no one would sense him.

"I'll leave the briefcase in the room," Ariabella said.

"I'll wire the fee to your account."

"Now that we have a picture of Val D'Esta, no one can lie to me. I'll know who was with him the moment they see his face."

The man slowed his pace and Judah anticipated his stop. He quickly leaned up against a wall and pretended to read his paper.

The tall man gently touched Ariabella's arm. "*Jane*, I think you should let the police handle it from here. No more interrogations. The lead detective has his suspicions and it's getting too dangerous."

"We have to catch him, Edgar. You know that. This is so much more than human trafficking. You heard that scumbag in there." She pointed over her shoulder. "He's doing horrible things to the people he takes. Besides, Val D'Esta is securing his compounds, making sure all his cargo is safe. That terminology alone is enough to give me nightmares. He's not in the country right now."

"That doesn't matter, and you know it." Edgar glanced over the streets and urged Ariabella to keep walking. "Val D'Esta's men are everywhere. Human and Olympian."

Judah perked up even more. It was one thing to have a human causing trouble; it was something entirely different to have an Olympian in the mix. Ariabella was talented at disguising herself to human eyes, even though he could feel the tiniest hint of her aura under her shields.

She wasn't strong enough to protect herself from an Olympian attacker.

"Please, Jane. Make this your last trip here." Edgar, whose name probably wasn't Edgar if he was calling her Jane, had a sincere expression of fear in his eyes. He cared for Ariabella and whatever they were involved in made him fear for her safety. "You're a talented woman, but you need more than talent to win this fight."

Ariabella nodded. "Okay, Edgar. I get it. How about this? I'll go change, you go change, and we can meet for lunch and you can show me pictures of those grandbabies I've heard so much about."

The dark-skinned man smiled. "Deal. I'll meet you over there in about half an hour, eh?" He nodded to the café where Judah had been sitting.

The two split ways and Judah followed Ariabella back to the hotel. He sat in a corner in the lobby until his bouncy blonde with her brightly colored bag came through, leaving the key to her room sitting at the front desk.

Judah could do one of two things: follow her to the café or see what was in that briefcase.

She had mentioned having a picture of Val D'Esta, and his gut told him it was in the room. Judah quickly swiped the key off the counter as the receptionist waited on another customer.

He made his way up to the room and inside, careful to avoid showing his face to the security cameras. Not that they would recognize him with his gray beard, hat, and hobble.

The hotel room was perfectly cleaned, not so much as a tissue out of place. Judah searched in the obvious places: under the bed, under the mattresses, bathroom, cabinets, television stand, nightstands, even the fridge. The vents were too small. He checked nonetheless, then went to the closet and found it in a pillowcase, wrapped up in one of the spare blankets. No one would've ever seen it.

"Good girl." Judah was proud. With a little more training, she would make a damn talented spy.

With one of the many tools in his pocket, he picked the lock and opened the case. It was full of notes, files, and pictures that made his blood run cold. Judah's hand shook as he held up a picture of the notorious criminal, Julio Val D'Esta.

Judah knew him by a much different name, a name that made his knees weak and his stomach churn. He was suddenly lightheaded at the thought that Ariabella was going up against this man.

His cell phone rang, scaring the shit out of him. The phone number, too, gave him chills. How did they—

"Judah," said General Falcon. "Someone needs to speak to you."

"*Si*, uh, yes, sir." He had to remember to use English again. Being with Ariabella had made him default to Italian.

"Judah," said a soft but urgent feminine voice. "Now you know why you must protect her. He knows and he is coming for the girls. Go now."

"Where?"

"Anywhere. I will find you." The line went dead.

Judah put everything back in the briefcase and got the hell out of that room as soon as he could.

Ariabella was in more trouble than she realized.

CHAPTER SEVEN

J UDAH HAD NO CHOICE BUT TO FACE THE MUSIC. IF ARIABELLA'S LIFE was in danger, he had to get her to safety. There was no time left and he wouldn't gamble with the life of his woman.

After packing up the briefcase full of evidence, he rushed to where Ariabella and Edgar were supposed to meet for lunch. The café was small and most of it was street side dining. Yet they were nowhere to be found.

"Shit." A heavy bass drum beat in his chest, so loud it pulsed in his ears. Relief flooded him when he saw them in line to order food. He stashed the briefcase in a planter box under a bush and hobbled over. "Excuse me, is that you, Ariabella?"

Dark eyes narrowed at him then darted around the room.

"Si. Can I help—" She wouldn't recognize him in this disguise. His aura, however, would be familiar to her. He allowed some of it to slip out. Those intelligent eyes widened a fraction with recognition. "Oh, my goodness…uh, Uncle! I almost didn't recognize you. Your hair is longer than the last time I saw you." She tiptoed up to hug him. "What are you *doing*?" she whispered in his ear.

Judah played the part. "Hello, darling niece. I don't mean to intrude. When I saw you, I had to do a double take. How could my little Ariabella be in town and not tell her favorite uncle?"

"I'm so sorry." She flashed a bright, almost real, smile at him. "I came to have lunch with my work friend. Edgar, this is my uncle…" Her eyes darted around until they landed on a man working on his laptop. "Mack. Uncle Mack, this is Edgar."

They exchanged pleasantries and shook hands.

Judah put his hand on Ariabella's upper arm and squeezed, applying a bit more pressure than necessary. "It's fortuitus that I ran into you, my dear. Your aunt is quite ill. I came to get her medicine. As much as it pains me to interrupt your lunch, I could sure use some assistance, child."

"Oh, no." Edgar's sympathy was genuine as he bought the whole bit hook, line, and sinker.

Ariabella looked conflicted for a moment then nodded. "Of course, Uncle." She met Edgar's stare. "I'm sorry, do you mind postponing?"

Edgar waved her off. "Not at all. By all means, please go. I'm glad he recognized you."

"Oh! Thank you, sir." Judah reached out and shook his hand.

"Not a problem. I pray your wife feels better soon." Edgar smiled at Judah, then touched Ariabella's elbow. "Call me as soon as you get home."

"Absolutely. Thanks for being understanding, Edgar."

As they said their goodbyes and exited the restaurant, they both kept up the façade. Ariabella tucked her hand in the crook of Judah's elbow as if to help the old man walk. Judah hobbled out to the sidewalk and turned the corner to retrieve the briefcase.

"What in the name of the gods are you doing here, Judah?" Words spit through clenched teeth, even as she smiled at a passerby.

"I could ask you the same question, *Jane*." He matched her snippy tone.

The use of her alias made her head whip towards him. Only then did she see what he held. "The briefcase, how did you find it? How do you know—"

"Shh." Judah glanced around and made sure no one was paying them much attention. "I'll explain everything when it's safe. We have to move. We have to leave, now."

She reached for the case. "You can't—"

"I can and I have. Come on." He put his hand on her back to urge her forward, towards a free taxi.

Her heels dug in like a stubborn mule's. This was a side of her he'd never seen before. "I have a driver, a special one. He knows to take different routes every time he drives me home. We should wait for him." She tried to push him off and walk on her own, yet he didn't let her go.

"We don't have time."

"He's one of us." The heat in her tone was hard to ignore.

While he knew this was what she wanted, he also knew what his mysterious caller had warned. Judah debated. "Fine. Call him."

Within seconds, her driver was there. He didn't ask questions; he didn't say a word. The taxi shot through traffic and out of the city before Judah realized it. His main focus was on Ariabella. She huddled to one side of the car, far away from him. Her whole body trembled and Judah reached for her, only to have her flinch at his touch.

"You can be angry later. Right now, you must be compliant. I have to get you out of the city and away from danger."

"You have a lot of explaining to do," she growled through clenched teeth.

Judah nodded. "Yes. I do. And if you get desperate enough, I imagine you can pull it out of me." He touched her cheek and she flinched, breaking his heart. "I'm hoping you will give me the chance to explain on my own."

Ariabella's tear-filled eyes met his. "How did you know where I was? Did you follow me?"

"Yes." He was already lining up a safe-house from his phone.

"Why?" She whispered her question.

He kept typing on this phone, sending the information to General Falcon. "Because I knew you were lying to me this morning."

"How?"

"You're clever, my love, but I've been doing this a long time. I knew a man called you, unless your girlfriend takes testosterone. That was my first hint. Second, was that bag." He motioned his chin in the general direction of her tote.

Ariabella scowled at her bright, frilly bag.

Judah read the confusion on her face. "You've never used it, not once since we've been together, yet you didn't need to pack anything fresh in it this morning. No wallet, no make-up, not even your favorite lip gloss that you use every day. Nothing. Which means you already had all that packed. I'm guessing there's a fake ID and credit cards in there. Nothing that can tie Jane to you."

Clearly pissed at her own oversight, Ariabella kicked at her bag and cursed under her breath. He'd never seen her angry or frustrated and he found this part of her made him sad. His Ariabella was sunshine and laughter. Her nature was to be jubilant. Seeing her so upset and off balance hurt his heart.

"Who were you interrogating this time?"

"None of your business." Her eyes flickered to their driver and back to him.

Judah nodded. This conversation would have to take place when they were alone. "I love you, Bella. More than you will ever know. I want you to remember that. Everything I do is because I love you."

"I'm sorry if I don't believe that right now."

"You lied to me as well." Not that it compared to all his many lies.

"This is what I do. This is how I use my gift to help people. If you knew, you wouldn't have let me go."

"I did know. I've always known."

Her head whipped around to him so fast, her blonde hair fell across her shoulder. "*Cosa?*"

Judah reached for her arm and pulled her towards him. Ariabella tried to resist, tears welling up in her eyes. Thracian strength won out and he pulled her back to his chest, wrapping his arms around her torso, not too tight, just enough that she couldn't wiggle away. Lowering his voice to whisper in her ear, he confessed his sins.

"A few weeks ago, I had just returned from a mission and was ready to take a couple months of leave. It was a hard assignment. I had to silence an Olympian who was getting too conspicuous. Humans were seeing things they shouldn't and asking questions that they don't ever need the answer to. It was…difficult for me…being that deep undercover. I needed time to process, time to get my mind right again. Not long after I returned home, a call came in, telling me that I had another assignment, off the books. I didn't want to take it, but it seemed simple enough and I got to take a free trip to Rome."

Ariabella went even more rigid in his arms and he held her tighter.

"I was to watch over a woman, to keep her safe, to make sure that no harm came to her as she went about her life. Simple enough. The minute I saw the picture of my mark, I knew I was in over my head. She was the most alluring woman I had ever laid eyes on. In all my years on this earth, I had never been…*moved*… by a smile, a face."

"No, Judah. I don't believe you." Ariabella shook her head and pushed against him. Her attempts were half-hearted. He couldn't let her go. If he did, she might not ever listen to him again.

"Please, let me finish. As soon as I saw you in person, I fell. You were in the market, picking out flowers. So beautiful. More lovely than any of the blooms you chose. You were sunshine and warmth and life; everything I had never known. The first time I heard you laugh—" He sighed and shook his head. Moisture fell from her eyes onto his arms. "There are no bells, no instruments, no angels in the Heavens who could make a purer sound than your laugh, Ariabella. I had to brace myself on a wall. I was so mesmerized, my knees shook."

"Stop it, Judah. You lie." She shook her head and leaned forward, trying again to break his hold. Judah wasn't going to let her slip away. He opened his aura to her and showed her all the emotions within him.

"You know I'm not. You know me, the real me, better than

anyone else. I've never been able to be myself, Bella. Not until I met you."

She shook her head, even though she knew he was right.

Judah continued, "For weeks, I purposely did things to make you see me. All my life, I've lived in the shadows. I'm good at being a shadow, a ghost. There one minute and gone the next. You? Gods, how I wanted you to see me—the *real* me. I prayed that you would notice me as a man, that you would make contact with me somehow so I didn't have to keep my distance. Every day that passed, every detail I discovered about your life made me want to be a part of your world.

"When you sat down in the square and read that letter, I couldn't hold it in any longer. There was this compulsion to speak to you, to have you notice me, talk to me. As soon as you did, I was yours. Mission or not, danger or not, I was sunk."

"You lie," she cried softly. "It's all a lie."

"I love you more than my own life, Ariabella. Ask me, use your powers. Do it. You'll see how I love you."

"No. You've lied to me all along and this is another tale, another manipulation."

Judah turned her around and gently tangled his fingers in her silken hair and pulled back so her face lifted. The tears in her eyes and the doubt on her face made him wish he could keep her in the dark about all of it. "And when we made love? Did that feel like a lie? Did you feel deceived when I was inside you, Bella? No. You felt my love, my hunger, my worship." He crushed his mouth to hers and kissed her with that same hunger. Only this time, he had something to prove.

Ariabella didn't melt into his kiss.

She didn't move her lips with his.

With force, she pushed at his chest and broke his hold. She

stared right into his eyes and propelled her aura until it consumed him. "Judah, tell me the truth."

For once, he was thankful for her compulsion.

⟡

Ariabella pushed her powers and aura into Judah so potently, his arms went slack and his eyes glazed over. She'd never used her powers so forcefully before.

"How long have you been watching me?"

"I was sent to Italy as soon as the Deities ascended to the Heavens. Four weeks prior to when I first spoke to you."

"Who sent you?"

"A woman. General Falcon made the assignment originally. Now I think he's under someone else's orders."

That didn't tell her anything. What woman could have more authority than the General? Then again, her brother was in good standing with the American General. Maybe it was Dante or someone he worked for? Maybe her brother knew something she didn't. "Why me?"

"They said you were special to someone very powerful and had to remain safe." Judah blinked, the only sign of his awareness.

"Safe from who? From what? Val D'Esta?"

"They didn't tell me."

"Did they give you hints, clues, anything?"

"No."

Ariabella's efforts weren't actually getting her answers. She sat back in frustration, gritting her teeth. If she didn't get the right answers, it was usually because she wasn't asking the right questions. Her eyes flickered to the brown case on the floorboard next to her bag.

"Why do you have the briefcase?"

"It holds the evidence I need to give to Master Ryse Castille."

Ryse Castille? The Master Thracian? What the *hell* was she into?

"Evidence of what?"

"To identify the person who is kidnapping Olympians." Judah stared into space, his brain signals waiting for her next command.

"Why are you in a rush to get me out of town?"

"The lady who sent me knew the moment I saw the evidence in the briefcase. She called to inform me that he knows who you are and he's coming for you and Bridget."

"Bridget?" Ariabella's pulse spiked and her mind raced. How could anyone know that Jane, her alias, and Bridget were associated? It was impossible. She and Edgar had worked tirelessly to separate Jane from her real identity. Her alias was flawless, right down to the forged medical records as a child. Who could possibly know her true identity?

"She said the *girls* were in danger. I assumed she meant you and Bridget."

So maybe he was wrong? As much as she didn't want to admit it, she needed Judah to give her answers on his own. Before she dropped her compulsion, she had one final question.

"Are you in love with me?"

"Beyond measure."

She clenched her eyes closed, wishing she could deny the truth. His betrayal hurt more because of his love. Hadn't that been what Hera had warned her about? *The truth you seek is still truth, though your perception is skewed.* Was this what the goddess meant? That even though her heart was broken that Judah would deceive her, his love was still true? Hera warned her that they had to face challenges together and keep the faith.

A hand touched hers and she popped her head up to look into Judah's hazy eyes. "I would give my life for you."

Ariabella retracted her aura and released him from her spell. He blinked a few times to clear the fog. When he did, he cupped her face with his palms. "Satisfied? I love you. I'll do anything it takes to keep you safe. I'm sorry I had to deceive you. That was my job. No more. As Zeus, and Ares, and Hera as my witnesses, I love you, Bella. You must believe me."

Anger gave way to the need for safety in his arms. "Judah." She fell against his chest and fisted her hand in his shirt. "I don't know how to handle this."

"We handle it together." His words echoed those of Hera and she allowed herself to believe that even though the two of them had much to work out, the gods meant for them to be together. She remained curled next to his body for the remainder of the trip. Judah held her tight and pressed kisses to her hair every few moments.

Once the taxi was parked outside of her building, Judah pulled his gun and chambered a round. "You stay in the car until I come back for you." He pinned the driver with a hard glare. "If you hear shots or see anything suspicious, you get her the hell out of here. I'll call with a location when I can. You just drive."

"Judah?" Ariabella touched his face. "I'm scared."

"It's okay. I'm going to clear the place before you go in." He kissed her then slid out of the car and into the apartment building.

Moments passed and the clock on the dashboard seemed to never change.

The taxi driver met her eyes in the mirror and shrugged. "What do you think, miss?"

Ariabella's stomach tossed and churned. She hadn't taken a full breath since he'd disappeared through the door of her building.

How long was too long? What if something had happened? Should she go in? He told her to stay in the car, but what if something had happened and he needed her?

She reached for the door handle and found the door of the taxi opened from the outside. A man rushed into the taxi and grabbed her by the throat. The driver tried to reach around and fight him off.

Ariabella screamed and grabbed at her attacker's hands. She looked into his black, soulless eyes and knew she'd made a grave mistake in returning to her home.

"Hello, Ariabella. Your father sent me." He pulled a gun on the taxi driver and shot him in the head. "It best not to fight me. Your sister is waiting in van."

Wheels screeched outside the taxi and he yanked her out of the car and into the street, grabbing the briefcase full of evidence. Ariabella kicked and screamed, wondering why no one was helping her. Where was Judah? Was he dead? Had this madman gotten to him first?

He dragged her by her hair into the dark van where two more men waited. He spit out orders in what she recognized as Russian and one of the men grabbed a role of thick, gray tape.

Despite her small size, she was able to kick and wiggle, making it harder for them to tie her down. It wasn't enough. The two brutes had her hands, feet, and mouth taped in no time. Tears fell down her face and her heart rapidly beat in terror.

Her captor sat across the van from her, staring at the way her dress was stuck around her waist, revealing her thigh and some of her panties. She had no way to cover herself. His eyes narrowed and he reached for her thigh. Ariabella screamed against the tape.

A woman yelled at him from the front seat. She climbed into the back, continually griping at the men in Russian. He pointed to Ariabella's thigh. Whatever he said didn't matter to the woman, who seemed to have more authority. She slapped away his hand and stuck a warning finger in his face, growling out orders. The woman smoothed down Ariabella's dress so that it wasn't hiked up to her hips. As if to make sure the man didn't try anything, she sent him to the passenger's seat of the van and she took his place on the opposite wheel well.

Wherever they were going, they were going in a hurry. It was all she could do to steady herself on the wheel well. She pitched to the right, fell off, and smacked right into Bridget. Once her eyes adjusted to the dark interior, she noticed her sister's eyes and mouth were covered and her hands were also tied. Whoever her captors were, they knew exactly how to disable their Olympian powers. Bridget was much more of a fighter than Ariabella, yet she needed her hands and sight to control the wind as a weapon. Ariabella's only firepower was her mouth, and it was taped.

"Stop fretting, girls," said the woman, her thick Russian accent making the broken English hard for her to understand. "We take you to your father."

Ariabella nodded, feeling no more safe at that proclamation, though she didn't fight the woman.

Hot, angry tears fell down her cheeks. If she and Bridget were both being kidnapped, then Judah was surely dead. The thought crushed her soul. Gods, how she loved him. And he loved her as fiercely. He would never allow anyone to hurt her if he were able to stop them…which meant he wasn't able to.

CHAPTER EIGHT

As soon as Judah stepped over the threshold, a bullet pierced his chest and nicked his heart; another went straight through his lung. There was no time to react to the invader's presence. No time to return fire. He simply dropped to the floor.

A man he didn't recognize stood over his body as he coughed up blood. Then Judah realized he had seen this man. The day of the execution. He was in the arena with another woman. This was the tail Maxim had placed on the girls.

"You are losing your touch, Judah." His thick Russian accent made every word more menacing. "I have been watching you for weeks. If my orders had been different, you would've been dead already. You are lucky to last this long."

The shooter stepped over his body and only paused when Judah grabbed his pants leg.

As hard as he tried, he couldn't get Ariabella's name formed. He only choked and wheezed; blood bubbled from his mouth. The once frantic beat of his heart now propelled his life's blood faster out of his chest. With every beat, every double thump of the drum pounding loudly in his head, he edged quickly towards death.

Thump-thump. Thump-thump. Thump-thump. Thump-thump. Thump-thump.

"Don't worry about the girl. Maxim will take care of her," the man sneered as he exited the apartment. His smirk and dark chuckle made Judah fear for his beloved Ariabella.

Thump-thump. Thump-thump. Thump-thump. Thump-thump. Thump-thump.

He had failed her.

Thump-thump. Thump-thump. Thump-thump. Thump-thump.

He had failed his mission.

Thump-thump. Thump-thump. Thump-thump.

He would die here and Ariabella would suffer in the hands of Maxim the Magician.

Thump-thump. Thump-thump.

With his last thoughts, he pleaded not for himself and for his life, but for Ariabella. *Gods of Olympus…Hera…please…save her.*

Thump-thump.

From a great distance away, an angel with dark eyes and dark hair, glowing with white light and bathed in the warmth of the gods, called to him. "Hold on, Judah. Stay with me."

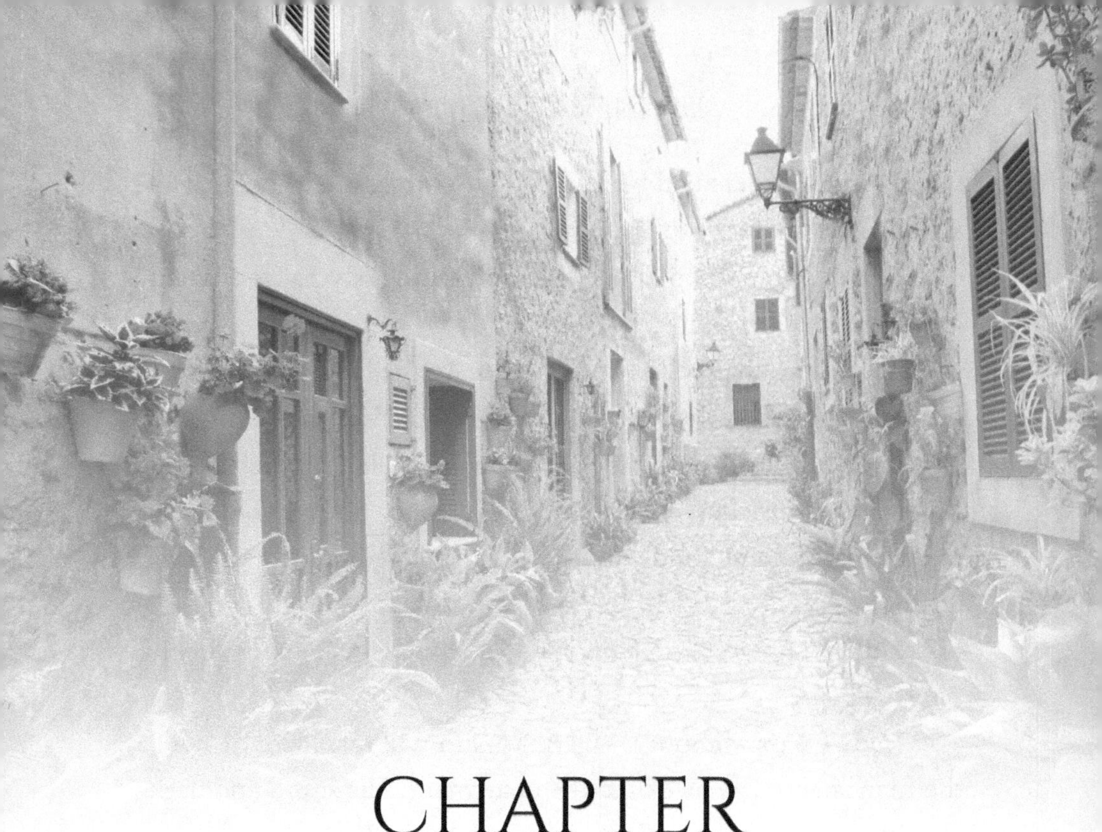

CHAPTER NINE

ARIABELLA HAD FRACTIONALLY REINED IN HER FEAR WHEN THE van stopped and the men threw open the back doors. After being in the dark van, the bright daylight sun made it hard to see. The Russians unloaded them from the van. Once her eyes adjusted, she could see they were at an airport.

Oh no.

Once they stepped foot on that plane, they could be shipped off to anywhere. How would she be able to call for help? Who would she call? Dante, perhaps?

Painted on the side of the small plane was the sigil of the European Deities, the house of the Avondales. Were the Russians telling the truth? Were they truly taking the girls to their father?

Could all the drama of being kidnapped simply be because her father was being secretive? Gods, she hoped so.

One of the men holding her spoke in Russian and pointed his chin at a black-haired woman talking to the pilot. He seemed agitated at the delay and none of his companions could answer him. They kept the girls partially hidden behind the van, as if to keep the woman, who must've worked for the airport, from spying them.

Once the pilot shook hands with the woman, he signaled to bring the girls aboard. The black-headed woman walked away. When she was nearly to the hangar, she glanced over her shoulder. Ariabella's heart flipped as the woman gave her a curt nod, as if to tell her, *I know*. There was something familiar about the woman. The connection escaped Ariabella's mind. What she did see was the sprig of bright red hair that had escaped as the wind caught the woman's hair. It was a wig. The woman quickly tucked in the red strands and hurried away.

Where had she seen this woman before? Why was she familiar, and why did Ariabella feel hope from that one knowing look?

They boarded the plane and the female Russian seated both her and Bridget, buckling them in like children. She met Ariabella's eyes and gave her a slight sympathetic smile. It didn't make Ariabella feel any better. Kidnapped was kidnapped.

And Judah. Ariabella clenched her eyes closed and tears streamed down her face.

Oh! Dearest Hera, please save Judah. Let him be alive. Please, gods, please save him.

The plane taxied down the runway and lifted into the sky. As it banked, Ariabella saw the land give way to water. She tried to focus on her location. They had been in the van for fifteen or twenty minutes at the most. There weren't too many airports close to the water within that drivetime from her apartment. It had to be Fiumicino airport. The land slowly faded from sight, putting more distance between her and Judah.

"You rest," the woman said. "The flight is hour and half." She sat in her own seat and gazed out the window like it was a normal day for her. Did this woman have to kidnap people that often in her line of work? *Santo Zeus.*

During the flight, Ariabella's mind raced with how everything had gone so wrong. Had it not been precisely that morning that Judah had kissed her and teased her, brought her body to a fever pitch by loving on her? She never should've left the apartment. Why didn't she heed her brother's advice and get the hell out of town? If Edgar hadn't called, maybe she would've. Her intention was not to let her partner down.

Oh no! What if something happened to Edgar? If these people knew of her alias, what if they also knew of his? Had she put his life in danger too? If only she had not been so stubborn…

Beside her, Bridget coughed against the tape on her mouth until it sounded like she might choke. Her face turned blue and she wheezed as she struggled to breathe.

Ariabella met the eyes of the Russian woman and pleaded with her to help Bridget. After a moment of indecision, the woman ripped the tape off her sister's mouth and Bridget sucked in air as if she'd been drowning. She coughed and then took more deep breaths.

"Water, please," Bridget begged and coughed more.

The female Russian narrowed her eyes, and for a moment, Ariabella feared she wouldn't help Bridget. Finally, she spoke to her companion. He answered without lifting his eyes from the magazine in his hands. The woman pursed her lips and nodded. "I get water."

"Please, please." Bridget coughed again.

As the woman walked away, Bridget whispered, "Aria, is that you?"

"Mm-hmm," she mumbled against the tape on her mouth.

"Is Judah…is Judah…*dead*?"

"Mm-hmm." Ariabella didn't want to answer positively. Unfortunately, Bridget had to know the chances of ever seeing him again were slim.

"Oh gods, no." Bridget began to cry softly as the woman returned with a Styrofoam cup of water. She stuck the straw in Bridget's mouth and her sister drank it down. When she was done, she thanked the woman for the drink.

Moving the cup to Ariabella, she lifted her brows as to offer her a drink.

Ariabella shook her head, not because she wasn't thirsty, but because she feared what would happen the moment she needed to use the restroom. Would the woman help her? Or would Mr. Grab-hands take over?

She leaned over and put her head on Bridget's shoulder to offer her some comfort. Bridget kissed her sister's hair and leaned her cheek against it. "I'm so sorry, Ariabella. This is all my fault."

Ariabella tensed. *What in the world did that mean?*

⸺ ⚭ ⸺

When one's sister was an Air Elementalist, plane landings were often smooth and incredibly bump-free…unless that sister had her eyes covered and her hands bound, effectively rendering her powerless to control a plane. The small private jet bounced and hopped to a landing, making Ariabella's already frayed nerves nearly snap.

The Russian man glanced back at his female companion and the two girls. "Is not good pilot," he said with a bored shrug. Was this guy seriously making small talk now when he had put a bullet through the head of her driver only a couple hours before? How heartless were these people?

As soon as the wheels were chocked and the plan engines died down, the Russians had the girls up and moving. Bridget tripped on the first step of the plane and nearly took the man down the stairs with her.

"Watch where you going," he shouted, catching himself on the rails.

"In case you forgot," her sister snapped, "my eyes are covered!"

The woman grabbed her arm and lifted her up. "Hush, girl, or your mouth will be too."

"Even blindfolded, I can see who the brains of the operation is."

Ariabella groaned as her sister smarted off to their captors. Classic Bridget. Only right now, Ariabella wished she would keep her lips locked shut.

Only when she made it down the stairs and onto the pavement did she glance around to see where they were. The airport was unfamiliar and busy. They had taxied over to a series of private hangars where—

The air left her lungs.

Her heart clenched in her chest.

Sweat formed on her forehead.

Her feet stuck to the ground.

No! This couldn't be happening!

Leaning against a black SUV, eyeing her with maleficent hatred and a baleful grin, was the one and only Julio Val D'Esta.

Any hope that she and Bridget might make it out alive died in her chest like a spent match.

Val D'Esta. The trafficking terrorist she'd been hunting for months. The man whose face she saw in a picture for the first time today now stood before her.

"Hello, Ariabella. Or is it *Jane?*" He smirked, completely unaffected by her presence, mocking even.

"I—I know that voice," Bridget said softly. She shivered.

"Yes, pretty girl. We met at the club." He reached up and trailed his filthy hands down her sister's face and Ariabella wanted to chop off his fingers.

Bridget blanched, "M-m-max?"

"I have many names, pretty girl. Some know me as Val D'Esta." He threw that remark at Ariabella like it was yesterday's news, laughing at her, "Most Olympians know me as Maxim." Once again, he tried to pet her sister, making Ariabella's blood boil. "Come, my pretty pet, your father is anxious to see you."

A realization hit her with the force of a turbo jet. All this time, for months and months, she thought she was so smart, so slick with her disguises and her fail-proof alias…she'd been nothing but an amateur, playing cards at a table with sharks. Maxim had been onto her since the night she and Judah went dancing. He had purposely approached Bridget. Val D'Esta, Maxim, whoever he wanted to be, was two steps ahead of her the whole time. Hell, he probably staged her interview this morning simply so he could abduct her.

Perhaps he hadn't counted on Judah being there. Either way, this vile man pushing her into the SUV had played her like a violin and her stupidity was the cause of Judah's death. Leaning her head against the window, she resigned herself to the fact that she might be joining her sweet Judah in the afterlife shortly.

At least she could hold on to that hope.

Spare moments later, the car stopped in front of a huge

warehouse. There was a thickness to the air, something ominous and vile coating the area. Ariabella didn't want to get out of the car. They left her no choice. The urge to flee had her feet moving away from the warehouse.

"No, you go this way." Maxim grabbed her shoulders and pushed her forward.

They climbed a tall, rickety set of metal stairs to an exterior entrance on the second or third story. With every step, bile rose in her throat. *Run!* her mind told her. Where could she go? How would she get Bridget?

It took a couple of seconds for her eyes to adjust to the darkness as she stepped over the high threshold and into the warehouse. Her eyes adjusted to the darker space and her stomach sank.

Santa Hera!

They stood on a landing, leading to a catwalk over the warehouse floor, where hundreds of people were attached to machines like batteries. It was a scene from a space alien movie, right in front of her eyes. These were some of the people Maxim had taken over the years. They were being used as lab rats.

"Welcome to the future of our race, my daughters." Ariabella's head whipped around to see her father approach, his chin held high as he motioned to the poor souls below.

"Daddy?" Bridget whispered, her voice shaky. "Daddy, help us."

Xavier pulled Bridget under his arm and reached to touch Ariabella's shoulder. "Don't worry, girls. You're safe with me."

Bridget leaned against Xavier for support, receiving a kiss on the temple from their father. As much as she wanted to, Ariabella couldn't find comfort in her father's embrace. More than anything, she wanted her father to love and protect them. It didn't escape Ariabella that Xavier hadn't immediately removed their bindings or checked on their safety. If their own father kept the girls bound from using their Olympian powers, how safe could they possibly be? And if Xavier had aligned himself with Maxim, what kind of horrible things had her father done?

Ariabella glanced down at the poor souls hooked to the machines. Was that the fate that awaited her? Would her father sacrifice his own daughters for this version of the future?

Please, Hera, hear me. Save us.

From somewhere deep within her soul, given life by faith alone, Ariabella heard her reply from the same voice that had spoken to her in the Coliseum days ago.

Justice is close at hand. Be strong, my child.

TO BE CONTINUED...

Divine Justice

A Prince must die.

Ryse and Avery Castille have no choice but to deliver the gods' justice to Ashton Avondale. His list of treacheries grows daily. First, they must find him. Their search for Ashton and his warehouses of demon-Olympian hybrids takes them all over the globe. Thank the gods for a talented teleporter, their key in winning the battle. They will face new foes, old friends, and a world of chaos.

Hades has spoken. The god of the underworld wants what is his and he will show no mercy if he does not get it.

Avery's ability to absorb Olympian gifts is both her greatest weapon and the biggest risk to their people. Her tendency to find trouble guarantees that Ryse will have his hands full, not only with the enemy—but with his wife. It's up to Ryse, Avery, and their ever-growing team of Elite warriors to track a traitor, save those who have been taken, and prevent the rise of a demon army before Hades steps in. But this is war, and no one will walk away unscathed.

Avery is the spark that started the fire.

When the final battle is fought,

will her flames be their salvation

or their damnation?

"This is how all horror movies start," Keona whispered to Nikki, who pressed her lips into a thin smile. "Two idiots loyally follow a bigger idiot to an unknown location and the minority character gets killed. I'm screwed."

Nikki giggled. "At least you can blink out any time you want. I'm stuck with her."

Pointing a finger at Nikki, she nodded. "True."

"You two act like I can't hear you," Avery called over her shoulder, still stomping through the woods.

"No, we just don't *care* if you hear us," Keona retorted.

Avery gave her the finger. "I need to rethink my squad."

Keona and Nikki chuckled.

"What are we doing out here?" Nikki tilted her head and watched Avery as she turned around and faced them.

She pulled a knife from her belt and Keona groaned. "See, horror movie."

"I think the only way for us to beat Ashton is to quit fighting fair. He's using minute drops of demon blood to boost his powers, giving him a serious advantage. What advantages do we have?"

Keona and Nikki answered in rapid fire.

"A teleporter."

"A thousand Thracians."

"The *Master* Thracian."

"Philippe."

"Hammon's staff."

"Piper."

"A team of computer nerds hacking every system known to man."

Avery raised her hands. "Yes, yes, we have all that. But we also have…" She pointed both hands, one holding a knife, at her chest. "Me."

Keona exchanged a side glance with Nikki. It seemed neither was going to touch that.

"I can conjure things now as a result of Nikki's blood. So far, there have been no side effects—"

Nikki held up a stopping hand. "You set a cake and your hair on fire."

"At first. I have to learn to use the powers, duh. The gods created me to be a weapon. I need to be a fully loaded weapon; otherwise, I'm just another Helioan."

"I don't like where this is going." Keona took a step back.

"Having a teleporter is a massive advantage over the enemy. Imagine if we had two." Avery met Keona's eyes.

"Oh my. Bad idea." Nikki shook her head.

"No, no, no." Keona held up her palms and shook her head. "There are a billion ways this could go wrong and I will not spend the rest of my life hiding from your husband. We're finally on speaking terms."

Nikki interjected. "Avery, when we exchanged blood, Hayden was in control. It was all neat and tidy, clinical, in a contained space, and Ryse was there in case anything went wrong."

"Everything will be fine," Avery dismissed her.

"I would like to revisit the whole flaming cake point before we go any further. I may be darker-skinned, but I don't want to be burnt." Keona frowned.

"Listen." Avery sighed. "You two weren't there on that ship when Xavier opened fire and Ashton was mentally battling my husband for control of his body. He nearly won. I can't risk Ryse like that again."

"You were the one who was shot, not him," Keona argued.

"Yes, and if I had been able to teleport, I could've gotten all of us out of there in an instant."

"You still would've been shot!" Keona threw up her arms.

"Maybe not. Even if I was, I could zip right back here to a Paean. Once the crap hits the fan, you're gonna be runnin' around crazy and you can't be two places at once. You're good, but even you're not *that* good. If I could help, why wouldn't we at least try? What's the worst that could happen?"

Closing her eyes and shaking her head, Keona thought of ten things that could go wrong in the blink of an eye—this was Avery after all. "Do you want the possibilities in alphabetical or numerical order? Nikki, please help me out here. Talk some sense into her."

Rounded hazel eyes bounced between the two women. She opened her mouth, only sighing at first. "I can see how this could go wrong…"

"Thank you." At least someone saw reason.

"…and I could see how this could be another huge advantage over Ashton."

"What?"

"Ha," Avery snapped with a smug grin.

Nikki turned to Keona, who narrowed her eyes. "After a learning curve, Avery was able to conjure simple things. The more she practices with a power, the better she will become. The gods wouldn't have given her the ability to absorb powers if they didn't expect her to use them."

"We don't have time for trial and error," Keona said. "At any second, Ryse could page me and off I go. What happens if this genius teleports half her body to Russia while I'm gone?"

"Can Piper heal half a body?" Avery inquired, thinking out loud.

"We aren't going to test that," Keona yelled. "Are you insane?"

"I'm not going to do anything rash," Avery promised.

"Lying is a sin." Nikki shook her head.

Narrowing her eyes, Avery stuck out her tongue at Nikki. "I

promise that I will not attempt any teleportation until you have explained how to do it."

"I've been perfecting my teleporting skills my whole life and you want me to explain it to you, what, in a thirty-second commercial? No way." Keona crossed her arms over her chest and stood her ground.

Avery lifted her chin. "What if I'm with Piper and she's in danger; I can't fight them all off and we need to get out quick, but you can't get to us? Then what?"

Damn, she went there—she hit the one button that Keona couldn't refuse. There was nothing Keona wouldn't do for her sister.

She ground her teeth. "You're already playing by Ashton's rules. That's not fair at all."

"It's a real possibility, and you know it. We're both mated to the most powerful men on earth. What better targets than us?" Avery spoke calmly, rationally…and she knew the moment she won.

Without a word, she took out her knife and made a slide down her palm. Flipping the knife, she held the blade and offered the hilt to Keona.

"It might not work anyway," Nikki said. "It might not be enough blood."

"I guess we'll see." Keona sliced her palm and shook hands with Avery. "Red, you're my freaking witness that I did not want to do this. You better not throw me under the bus when this blows up in our face."

Nikki nodded.

The ladies stood there with hands clasped, blood mixing in their palms.

Nothing happened.

Keona shifted her eyes from Avery to Nikki and back. "How do you know if it worked?"

"I have to try to use the power."

"Not *yet*." Keona gripped her hand tight. "Don't let go of my hand until I say. At least if you teleport, I might make the trip with you."

Avery nodded, concentrating hard.

How in the hell was she going to boil down a lifetime of learning into a quick'n dirty lesson? If she didn't figure it out, Avery might be in big trouble. Their blood had mixed. Maybe it was enough, maybe it wasn't. Either way, it was too late to turn back now.

She took a deep breath and met Avery's eyes. *Gods, give me the right words.* "When teleporting, you have to focus on several different aspects of the move. First, where are you going? What do your surroundings look like? Buildings? Streets? Open fields? You must have a clear mental picture. What type of material will your feet land on? An asphalt road? A grass lawn? A concrete sidewalk? A wooden pier? You must set your mind to land on that surface." She stomped a foot for emphasis. "Otherwise, you'll end up fifty feet in the air, fall, and break your damn leg like I did when I was little."

"Is that what happened on the boat?" Avery asked.

"Yes, I was nervous and I didn't take the curvature of the earth into account. I saw the water and focused on the distance, not the destination and the landing. See what I'm saying?"

Avery nodded.

"Next, you have to think about what you're moving. Your body. Your clothes. Your shoes. Your weapons. For now, *please* don't try to take others with you. It will not end well. My mother had me practicing with mice and stray cats as a child. It took me a long time, years, to master moving other living organisms."

"What happened?" Nikki whispered.

"There were pieces missing. It was a bloody mess. Rather traumatic. I don't want to talk about it."

Avery and Nikki blanched.

"Noted." Avery nodded vigorously.

"Okay," Keona continued, "until you truly get a handle on this power, you need to keep your thoughts on a serious leash."

"I can do that. It's my mouth that needs a muzzle."

"I mean it, Avery. I have to be overly careful about wishing I was somewhere else, or thinking about a place I want to visit or a restaurant I want to dine in. I once blinked into a Macy's display window while thinking about a sweater I had fallen in love with. You have to be careful; you'll pop up wherever you want to go—and people tend to scream when you appear out of thin air."

Yeah, she didn't want to think about the commotion she had caused as a teenager…wishing to go to Times Square…forgetting to blink clothes with her. Keona shook her head. Nope. No one needed to know about that.

"Right. Destination. Landing. Accessories. Control my thoughts. Got it." Avery tried to pull away.

Keona hesitated. "I'm scared to let you go."

Avery took a deep breath. "I can do this."

Reluctantly, Keona released her hand and accepted a rag from Nikki. They wiped their palms and then stood there, waiting for something to happen.

"Should I try?"

"No."

"Yes."

Keona and Nikki answered at the same time.

"We'll never know if it worked, if you don't attempt it. Start small." Nikki glanced around and pointed off in the distance. "Try to go to that tree, the big one there."

Avery nodded and shook out her shoulders like a fighter in the ring. Closing her eyes, she stood still for several seconds.

Keona and Nikki stepped back, their feet crunching the fallen leaves.

They waited…

and waited…

Nothing.

Avery opened one eye. "Did I move?"

"Not even a hair on the wind," Keona answered, feeling slightly relieved. Maybe it didn't work? Hopefully, it didn't work.

"Perhaps it wasn't enough blood?" She shrugged. "Nikki and I did a full-on transfusion thanks to Hayden."

"Well, we tried. Better luck next time. Let's go." Turning on her heel, Keona headed back to the palace. "I'm kind of hungry. I didn't exactly get to eat with you earlier."

"Sorry you missed it," Nikki mumbled, face pointing to the ground.

Keona heard a tone there. Was that sarcasm? She didn't know Nikki well enough to tell, yet the redhead often gave off a vibe that she didn't care for Keona's presence. Which was weird, because nothing negative had ever passed between them—that she knew of.

While she was lost in that thought, Keona didn't hear what Avery prattled on about. She focused on their topic right in time.

"I took me forever to get my recipe right. Marshall's, a freakin' backwoods bar, had the best roast beef dinner you've ever put in your mouth. God, I miss it—"

Crap!

"Avery, don't think about—"

Keona's words cut off in time to see Avery's eyes roll back in her head and her body fall limp.

"What happened?" Nikki shrieked, rushing to her side to pick her head up off the ground.

"She's a mule, that's what. I told her *not* to think of locations."

Keona frantically checked for a pulse and breath. *Thank the gods.* "She's alive." When she opened Avery's eyelids, her eyes were solid white.

Nikki gasped; her voice rose an octave. "Why are her eyes like that?"

"I—I—I don't know!" Keona shook her shoulders. "Avery! Avery wake up!"

She didn't move.

"This is bad. This is really bad." Hazel eyes filled with fear met Keona's.

"I told you this was a bad idea. Ryse is going to have my head. I'm going to have to spend the rest of my life running from that scary mother fu—"

"Hey! That's my mate you're talking about."

Keona and Nikki both froze, their eyes darting down to the limp body and back to each other. Avery wasn't in there, however. The great power of her aura didn't emanate from the body. No, her aura came from behind them…and damn, did she *not* want to think about why.

"Avery," Nikki whispered loudly, her voice pitched high with stress.

"Uh, Houston, we have a problem."

Both women slowly turned their heads in the direction of the voice and the aura…to see nothing but forest.

Yeah, they had a big effing problem alright.

ABOUT THE AUTHOR

 JoAnna Grace lives in a world of alpha males and strong females where true love conquers all—at least in her books! From the time she started holding a crayon she began to create magical worlds. Living in the real world was never an option. A proud indie, she has published over a dozen novels including The Divine Chronicles series, The Blake Pride series, Riverview Romances, and more. This writer loves to read contemporary, paranormal, and urban fantasy romance novels.

JoAnna's tales are spun at her home in East Texas where she lives with her Prince Charming, three kids, and a few dogs and cats. When not hiding behind the computer screen chugging coffee, you can find her having fun with family and friends, singing, camping, or managing multiple businesses.

Connect on social media!

Like, Follow, Tag Jo, and share this book with your friends.

Instagram @authorjoannagrace
Facebook @joannagraceauthor
Goodreads: goodreads.com/author/show/7173373.
JoAnna_Grace
Bookbub: www.bookbub.com/profile/joanna-grace

Make sure you're in the know. Sign up for the newsletter today!
http://eepurl.com/B_DM5

Do you want to help an author? Leave a review
Your opinion matters.
Every review can help.